Alpha's Mate

Bad Boy Bears
Book 2

Renee Rose

Lee Savino

Midnight
ROMANCE

Author's Note

Shout out to Missy F., an amazing reader and superfan of the Bad Boy Alpha books! She backed our Bad Boy Alpha Kickstarter and sponsored the character Missy. And she instructed us to "not hold back!" So get ready for Axel and Missy's book next in a Bad Boy Bear series!

Want FREE books?

Receive a slew of free Renee Rose books: Go to **http://subscribepage.com/alphastemp** to sign up for Renee Rose's newsletter and receive free books. In addition to the free stories and bonus material, you will also get special pricing, exclusive previews and news of new releases.

Did you know you can buy direct from Renee Rose? Get signed books, special editions, and heavily discounted bundles. Use this coupon for an additional 10% discount on your entire order - **READER10** or go here https://shop. reneeroseromance.com/discount/READER10

Download a free Lee Savino book from www. leesavino.com

Did you know you can buy direct from Lee Savino? Get special editions and heavily discounted bundles. Use this coupon for an additional 10% discount on your entire order - **READER10 or** click here **https://leesavino. myshopify.com/discount/READER10**

Chapter One

Matthias

There are worse ways to torture a man than making him a doctor in a small town where his fated mate is off-limits.

I just haven't found one yet.

It's five thirty-two on a Monday night, and the mayor of Bad Bear Mountain's blowing up my phone. Daisy's called six times in the past two hours, probably to pick my brain about the Bad Bear Winterfest.

Fates, I need to avoid her. Not because I don't want to get pulled into planning a small town festival–although I don't. But because of Daisy's delectable granddaughter.

Maisy. My sweet mate.

No, don't think about her.

On long days like these, it's hard to keep my thoughts from straying to her. I just did a double shift at the hospital in Santa Fe, and drove home only to swing by here to cover the rest of the nurse practitioner's shift here at the clinic. I'm not tired; my shifter side has too much stamina for that. I mean, I could sleep. But I really need to go outside. My

1

bear wants some forest time, and keeping him from going feral is a constant pressure.

Sometimes, I think I work all the time just so that when I finally go to sleep, I'm too tired to dream of *her*.

I run my hand over my face.

The scent of mulled cider and caramel apples wafts through the door, and my bear instantly surges to the surface.

At first, I think I'm imagining it because when I let my mind wander, all I think of is her. Her hair, her scent, her smile, the delicious curves she hides under slightly too-baggy clothes.

But then, I realize...

She's here.

Fuck.

I can't stop myself from sucking the scent in through my nostrils, savoring the notes of caramel and cinnamon and delectable young female.

I groan. The smell makes my mouth water. My dick gets hard. My fangs try to punch through my gums, lengthening and ready to sink into something sweet.

Nope.

Not happening.

That can never happen.

I yank open the drawer of my desk where I keep the vials of Moon Cure. It's a special formulation I came up with to deal with my...unique situation. I rip open a fresh syringe and fill it. I don't even bother to sanitize the top of the bottle or my skin. I jab it into my biceps and press the plunger down.

The cooling sensation spreads through my arm. Sweet relief, just in time. In a few seconds, it'll bring a dullness to my senses. Like bringing a curtain up between my rational brain and my desires. My logical self and my feral one.

My bear doesn't like it, but he understands.

There's a knock on my office door.

I withdraw the needle as I shove my desk drawer closed, then drop the needle in the trash can. I'll put it in the biohazard box later. "Yes, Sara?"

Sara opens the door. "Dr. Matthias? We have a walk-in."

Yes. I'm well aware. And I know exactly who it is.

"The patient hoped to see Nancy, but she just left."

I stand. "It's okay. Nancy left early to see her son in the school play. I'm covering her patients 'til closing." I straighten my glasses and give her a smile. "Show the patient to room two and let her know I'll be there in a moment."

Them. I should've said *them*, not *her.* I shouldn't know her gender when all Sara said was *patient.* I need to get my bear under control because I'm making mistakes.

"Right away, Doctor." Before Sara leaves, she whips out a cloth and polishes away an invisible speck of something from the doorknob. There's no dust in the entire clinic–everything is spic and span after the renovation, but it doesn't stop Sara from buffing doorknobs with a smile. She's proud of this place.

Residents of Bad Bear Mountain used to have to drive to Santa Fe for all healthcare needs until Bad Bear's formidable old mayor, Daisy, and I helped found this place. She badgered someone to donate this drafty old house, and I volunteered my hours along with a part-time nurse.

Now the newly renovated clinic is staffed with a full-time manager and nurse practitioner, all made possible by generous donations from Lana Langmeyer and Paloma Castillo, our resident billionaires.

I lean against my desk and draw in a steadying breath as I wait for the Moon Cure to flood my system. My bear sends me a flood of fast-motion images– me rushing into the exam room, throwing my beautiful young patient on the table, and feasting between her legs. Me holding her down and marking her savagely with my teeth. Me shifting to bear form, picking her up, and carrying her off to my den for an undisturbed ravishment.

Not. Happening. I tell him firmly, as I do every time I catch Maisy's sweet scent.

She's my greatest torture. My longest trial. Lately I've been allowing myself to stop into the cafe to get coffee before the drive to Santa Fe for a morning shift. That's when my willpower is at peak strength.

I don't dare get close to her otherwise. But today, I have no choice.

When I decide I'm steady enough, I head to the exam room. The caramel apple smell grows stronger in the hall.

My mouth waters.

My bear thrashes beneath the surface. This is more than hunger. It's a deep longing, a mad craving.

I won't give in.

The antique floors creak under my feet. My steps slow, and I check over my blue scrubs to make sure they're clean– I changed after my last shift, but it's a habit in case there's some blood spatter that might scare the patients.

I open the door and see the female I've sworn not to touch sitting on the examination table. Maisy Bennett, my impossibly young mate.

"Maisy?"

The beautiful human jerks in surprise. Her pink lips

4

part with a gasp as she teeters on the edge of the bed and starts to fall.

I always have this effect on her, my beautiful little klutz.

I'm across the room in a blur, moving with shifter speed in time to catch her in my arms. She fits perfectly. I shouldn't hold her so close, but I can't help it. It feels so right to hold her.

I've never been so close to her before. I've never allowed myself to touch her, even though I want her more than my next breath. Even though I dream about her every night. Spend most of my hours avoiding her and my obsessive thoughts about her.

"Doctor?" Her already pale skin leaches color, as if she's seen a ghost, but the scent of caramel and cinnamon blooms brighter.

My bear sucks it in like a drug. He tries to send the fast-forward images again, but I refuse to let him break the barrier in my brain.

"Are you okay?" I set her back on the patient bed, loosening my hold on her reluctantly.

"Mhmm," she mumbles, with her beautiful blue eyes fixed on the floor, and I'm reminded why I don't get close to Maisy Bennett. She's intimidated by me.

I step back, forcing the doctor in me to take over. My shifter senses note everything about her. Her color and temperature seem fine. Eyes are a bit dilated, but within normal range. Her pulse has sped up since I entered the room–I can hear it booming in my ear.

Her hand goes to her abdomen, and pain ripples across her face. I'm dying to pull her back into my arms and comfort her, but I force myself to act professional. I clear my throat. "What brings you in today?"

"Nothing." She tugs down her shirt, which is a cute

crop top sweater the exact color of her eyes. "I should go." She starts to slide off the table.

"Sit down," I order a bit too harshly for an ordinary patient. Her cheeks flush with color, but she immediately settles and puts her hands in her lap.

"Good girl."

Whoops. Did I really say that out loud? What am I doing? I can't talk to a patient this way.

Especially not this particular one. The mayor's grand-daughter. The girl I've been avoiding for so long—otherwise, I'd have her marked and bred with ten bear cubs by now.

But she reacts to the praise—sucking in a breath. Her scent—that incredible, delectable scent—grows stronger. My gums ache as my fangs descend. I turn away from her and grip the counter because the urge to pin her down and mark her is so overwhelming.

My bear roars with possessive triumph. He wants to touch her, hold her, protect her. My bear has a million dark and dirty things he wants to do to her.

I've got to get myself under control.

"I'm fine." She sounds a little breathless. Her cheeks pinken, and her pupils are blown—a sure sign of arousal. If I didn't know this from my medical training, I'd know it because I can smell all her secrets.

Does she like being called a good girl?

I want to make her *my* good girl. I want to carry her home, tie her to my bed, and feast between her legs. Train that intimidation right out of her and teach her she's more than safe with me. I'll take care of her every need. She'll obey my every order...

Fuck. No. That can't happen. I already know that can never happen. Maisy is far too young. She's in her early twenties, but I'm thirty-two and an authority figure in her life. I have power over her, power that it'd be wrong to exploit. She can't even look me in the eye without falling over. She definitely couldn't handle me or my bear. I'm way too much for her.

So I go dom-lite, fixing her with an authoritative gaze and a raised brow. "Maisy, you're in pain. You're not going anywhere until I figure out what's wrong."

* * *

Maisy

There are six things you should know about me:

1. I have PCOS
2. I make a mean spiced pumpkin latte–with real pumpkin as the OG recipe calls for
3. I run a coffee shop with my grandmother, Daisy
4. Yes, I drink waaaaay too much caffeine
5. I'm an avid reader and someday want to expand the cafe to add a bookstore and brewery
6. But Dr. Hunk–aka Matthias Stark–makes my heart beat faster than a venti blonde roast with quadruple espresso shots

Right now, I sit on the patient table, staring at the floor. If I look at the good doctor, I will spontaneously combust. I'm already hot all over, just from getting whiffs of his sophisticated cologne.

Be cool, be cool... whatever you do, don't drool!

He's wearing blue scrubs. Not the blue scrubs! Blue is a

calming color, but that's not how it affects me. His dark skin seems to glow against it, and the way his short sleeves show off his powerful biceps makes me feel like I have a heart condition.

Have you ever been around a guy so hot it destroys your brain? I live a pretty sheltered life on Bad Bear mountain. I don't really party. I perv on celebrities like everyone else, but Dr. Hunk is a real life celebrity—sexy, smart, perfect. After the Latte Incident where he said good morning, and I shouted "BLARG!" and spilled an entire oat milk latte on myself, I've learned to avoid him. So there is definitely no way I can have this conversation with *him*.

"I thought you'd be the nurse," I blurt.

"Nancy had to leave early. I can help you." He regards me with his dreamy brown eyes. His glasses only emphasize how gorgeous he is. He looks so collected and in control, but I know his secret. He's a bear shifter. Most of the residents of Bad Bear know that Winnie and the seven now-grown boys she adopted are different from the rest of us, but we protect that secret, and in return, they protect and give back to the town.

The fact that Dr. Hunk is a bear means he has a wild side. I wonder if he lets it out in the bedroom...

Gah! I need to stop perving on the good doctor. He's not an object of desire. It's not his fault he's perfect in every way.

"No. You can't." I tug on my shirt, pulling it down to hide my belly. Why, oh why did I wear a cropped sweater today of all days? One of my New Year's resolutions is to be braver. Another was making this health care appointment. Between running the cafe and helping my grandma, Daisy, with Winterfest, I don't really have time, but the pain has gotten unbearable.

He catches my hand, staying it. It's a light touch, but his big hand almost swallows mine. "Maisy, please." His other hand slides over my belly. It's warm, the touch sensual although I'm sure he doesn't mean it to be. "What hurts?" He slides his hand across my abdomen like he's soothing me.

I close my eyes. His sandalwood scent surrounds me, warm and comforting. I want to roll on my back and offer my belly to him like a puppy.

Yes, please. Please touch me more.

Crap, he asked me a question, and he's waiting for me to answer.

Eek. It took a lot for me to even come in today, and now I have to talk about my private parts with my long-time crush? "It's my ovaries."

"Are you on your period? Do you have cramps?"

"No, I just had my period a couple of weeks ago." I wave to my journal, where I chart my symptoms and cycle regularly. "I won't get it for a month or more. I'm not very regular. I have cysts. They hurt so bad, but… the Ob-Gyn says there's no way I could feel that."

His brow furrows. His hand still rests on my belly, and even though I'm in pain, I start imagining what would happen if he turned his fingers and slid them lower, between my legs.

"She's wrong. A lot of patients feel pain from ovarian cysts. It's very common."

He's so assuring, and I can't hold back anymore. The dam bursts. "She said I have PCOS, but there's no way I'd actually feel the cysts. She said I had to be imagining the pain. She said…" my voice catches, and I mumble the rest, feeling the tug of shame, "She said I just need to lose weight."

Dr. Hunk frowns, and it's chilling how handsome he is, even when he's stern. "She didn't prescribe something to manage your condition?"

I shake my head, feeling miserable.

For a second, his eyes blaze blue. It must be a bear thing. I've seen it before on Axel, his brother, and my pity prom date, but I don't know what it means. We don't know much about our, er, different neighbors, but we respect their privacy, and in return, they'd do anything for our little town.

"That's not okay." His voice is a guttural growl that sends goosebumps skittering up my arms. "You should never have to suffer like this."

I nod miserably. He's angry, but not at me.

"Maisy, listen to me." He takes both my hands now and faces me. He's so handsome I can barely look at him, but the moment feels more intimate than a doctor and patient. My shoulders relax for the first time in years. "One of the symptoms of PCOS is weight gain. There are ways to manage the symptoms, but our first priority is to address the pain. You don't need to lose weight. You need a better doctor. And it isn't your fault she was an idiot. And mean."

I nod, my eyes smarting with tears. Geez, I can't cry right now. I've already embarrassed myself enough around him.

But it feels so, so good to have someone listen to me. To have someone hear me out and rally to my side.

"You did a brave thing coming in today. Got that?"

I nod.

"I'm going to need to hear a *yes, Matthias*."

Oh, damn. He sounds like one of the dommy heroes from my favorite romance novels. His smile softens the command, but the order makes my pussy clench.

Does he have any idea of his effect on women when he uses that dominating tone?

I straighten my shoulders, feeling better. It's such a relief to have someone I trust listen to me, praise me, then tell me what to do. "Yes, doctor." I could never call him Matthias. I owe him too much respect.

He nods, and I hear the echo of *good girl* spoken in his deep voice, even though he doesn't say it.

"Here's what we're going to do," he starts, but a creaking floorboard interrupts him.

"Doctor?" the front desk manager calls from the hall. "Jasmine Wilkins is on the phone. She's freaking out. Oliver stuck a Lego up his nose."

Dr. Hunk clenches his jaw. He half turns to go but pauses like he doesn't want to leave.

"That sounds serious. You better go," I whisper. It'll give me a chance to run away and fake my death. I can't believe I ended up getting Dr. Hunk as my doctor when I came to talk about female trouble.

Ugh.

"Dr. Matthias?"

"I'm coming." His deep voice is so comforting. "Don't move," he orders me.

My pussy clenches again at his authoritative tone.

"I'll be right back."

I wait until the door closes behind him and slip off the bed. Time to make my escape. The clinic is in an old house. It's been renovated, but an old bathroom is attached to this patient room.

I waste no time ducking in there, unlatching the window, and shoving it up. After popping out the screen with two quick bangs of my fist, I stand on the toilet and hoist one leg over the windowsill.

I hear the deep rumble of Dr. Hunk's voice down the hall, and my nipples tighten.

Dear God, why does he have this effect on me? It's like I turn into a puddle of goo around him. It's so much better to avoid him than embarrass myself the way I do.

Ouch. Ouch, ouch, ouch. I sit on the window casing to swing my other leg through, then peer at the sloping ground beneath. It's a bit further down than it was on the inside, but I can jump.

The delicious notes of Dr. Hunk's voice cease. Oh God, he's coming back! It's now or never.

Thank you, Dr. Hunk, but I just can't discuss my female problems with you when being close to you makes me quiver like a Jello shot.

Please, forget you ever saw me here. And forget that my best friend and I call you Dr. Hunk behind your back.

I suck in a breath, hold it, and push off.

* * *

Matthias

It takes me two minutes to talk Jasmine through a Lego extraction on her five-year old, Oliver, and ten more minutes to calm her down.

My bear tugs on me the whole time, wanting me to get back to Maisy.

The caramel apple scent has faded by the time I walk down the hall, and I know before I open the door what happened.

Sure enough, there's a pink backpack decorated with a beaded daisy–Maisy's bag. But no sign of her.

My patient escaped.

This is exactly what I was afraid would happen. I've

tried to be calm and rein in my bear around her. She's already nervous around me. Whenever I get close, her cheeks flare with color, and she starts dropping things.

It's adorable.

Something in her bag buzzes. Her phone. I pull it out and see it's an unknown number with a Nevada area code. Looks like the same Nevada number has called her a bunch, too, but never left a message.

My bear growls. I don't like that someone's pestering her. Who would be calling her like this?

Now I'm snooping shamelessly. Her journal is here too, under her bag. It's open to a page where she's tracked her symptoms in neat script. The scientist in me admires her methodical tracking of her cycle and pain. There's enough data here for me to prescribe her pain meds immediately although I will schedule her for a nurse's appointment tomorrow for an examination. I'll make a note on Maisy's chart that I strongly recommend Nancy talk to her about getting on birth control to help manage her hormones.

That will be a start. It's not enough to satisfy my bear, but I can assure him we'll watch over her. She won't be in pain again, not on our watch.

My bear briefly recommends killing everyone who's treated her poorly, including the person blowing up her phone.

Maybe later, I will tell him. *We don't want to distress her any more than we already have.* Those are the magic words that get him to settle down.

Everything in me wants to read her journal, but it's wrong to violate her privacy. In a minute, I'll close it and put it in her bag. But first, I bring the paper to my nose and inhale her scent.

A piece of paper falls out and flutters to the floor. I pick it up and can't help glancing at the flowing script. She used a purple pen to write *New Year's Resolutions* at the top.

> *Glow up*
> *Dr. appointment for PCOS*
> *Plan DD expansion*
> *Set boundaries with Allen*

Set boundaries with Allen? Who the fuck is Allen, and why does she need to set boundaries with him?

My bear roars to the surface, ready to savage the guy who's upsetting my mate.

Then I remember something I learned in my extensive stalking of my gorgeous mate: Allen is the name of her father. He's a drug addict like her mom was. So, it makes sense she'd need to set boundaries with him. I make a mental note to find out what the asshole is doing to her right now that requires a better boundary.

Then I finish reading the last two items on her list:

> *Stand up for yourself!!! You can do it!*
> *Go on a date*

The second-to-last one on the list is underlined multiple times and makes me smile. My little human is being brave.

But it's the last one that gets me. I can't imagine her

asking someone out on a date–my bear won't allow me to even entertain the thought.

Maybe I can be her fairy godbear and make all her dreams come true.

No. No, I can't. It would push my control too far. Even with the Moon Cure. My lust for Maisy is still there, it's just muted. And when the dose wears off, my bear will be all the more wild.

I make a decision and pull out my phone. I can't call Maisy–she left her phone here, but she lives with her grand-mother, Daisy, who has been calling me nonstop since lunch.

"Dr. Matthias!" Daisy answers on the first ring. "I'm so glad you called me."

"Daisy, I need–" I try to take control of the conversation before she launches into planning the Bad Bear Winterfest.

"You need to see Maisy," she interrupts in a rush.

"What?" Daisy is the mayor of our small town, and every conversation I'd had with her in the past few years has been about either her health or some Bad Bear municipal crisis.

"She's been in so much pain. I've told her to go to the clinic, but she won't, and I think you need to do a house call–"

"I'm actually calling about Maisy. Is she with you?"

Daisy sucks in a breath. "Did she call you? Did you examine her? Do you–"

"That's confidential," I shut her down firmly. "Even if it wasn't a HIPAA violation, I'd never share a patient's medical information with anyone but them."

"But I'm her grandmother!"

"Daisy," I say in my doctor-dom voice. "Maisy is a

grown woman. She can make her own choices about her medical care."

Daisy sighs into the phone. "You're right." She sounds calmer. "I've just been so worried."

"Actually, I'm calling because I have Maisy's bag. She left it behind."

"At the clinic?" Daisy sounds hopeful. "Never mind, you can't tell me. She's here at the house. Got back a bit ago. You can drop it off."

"Will do." I say goodbye and hang up before Daisy starts rattling off Maisy's symptoms one by one. I've noticed that Daisy likes to be in charge and in everyone's business. It works for her as Mayor—she loves staying on top of all the town's gossip and genuinely wants to make Bad Bear a better place.

But it's not okay for her to run Maisy's life as well. I get the feeling that Maisy's lived in her namesake's shadow for too long.

But I'm no better, am I? It's bad enough that I read Maisy's journal. If my bear had his way, I'd take over her whole life.

And make it better, my bear whispers. It's a tempting thought.

But I can't. I slammed that door shut the moment I realized Maisy was my mate. When she was still a *teenager,* and I was a full-grown bear with some very dark desires.

Which is why I'm not suitable for Maisy.

I pick up Maisy's journal again and re-read the New Year's resolutions list.

Something about it makes my chest squeeze. She's so innocent. So pure.

I can't sully her.

She may be an adult now, but she's still fragile. Keeping

my distance is still best for both of us. She's always over-whelmed by my presence, and I need to keep my bear under control. The Moon Cure compound only works so well.

She needs us, my bear rumbles.

It's true. She's in pain, and she came to me. Sure, she meant to see the nurse, but Fate intervened and made sure she ended up in my arms. Now I can't forget how good it felt to have her there.

How right.

Except it's not right. A man like me—with tastes like mine—could so easily steamroll a sweet young woman like Maisy. And it would be a gross abuse of power.

So no. No matter how delicious it was to be the man in charge of Maisy for those few minutes I had her in my exam room—that role can never be mine.

At least not for many more years. Not until she's a confident, mature woman who knows what she wants and how to get it. If that ever happens. Then, if she chooses me, I'll unleash the feral part of me that wants to absolutely *consume* her.

Chapter Two

Maisy

That was the most embarrassing thing that has ever happened to me in the history of embarrassing. And that's saying something because situations like these are always happening to me.

It's more embarrassing than the time the school announced that I'd been voted Homecoming Queen. I'd gasped, stood up from the lunch table, and started to thank everyone who supported me, only to be informed that there'd been a mix-up, and my friend Missy Baptiste was actually Homecoming Queen. Which made more sense, seeing as Missy was actually popular and a beauty queen pageant winner.

It happened again in junior year when the drama club listed "Maisy Baptiste" on the posters for the lead of the school play. By then, I'd learned my lesson and knew better than to celebrate, and sure enough, it was a mix-up. I wasn't even in the play–just a stagehand, and the only reason I got that part was because Missy was my best friend.

No one ever wants me–they always want Missy. Or

they confuse Maisy with Daisy and get me mixed up with my grandmother.

The point is, there have been plenty of opportunities to graduate summa cum laude from the school of Mortifying Ordeals, and I have my degree.

But today I got my Ph.D. Not only did I end up telling my doctor crush–the hottest man in the state–about my awful ovaries, but I fell off the table, and he had to catch me.

Not that I minded getting swept up in his powerful arms.

I draw in a breath. I can still smell his cologne, notes of cedar and sandalwood. He touched me, and I keep reliving his hand stroking my belly.

I know it wasn't supposed to be erotic, but to me, it was the most sensual thing I've ever experienced. He's so big, he makes me feel petite. And beautiful. It was fun to imagine for a moment–me as the fairy-tale princess getting wooed by the handsome prince.

It's only a fantasy, but it sure feels good.

It's the only thing about today that isn't terrible. I am seriously thinking about faking my own death. Or at least running away from home.

I'm hiding in my bedroom when my grandma knocks on my door. "Maisy?"

"Come in." I'm lying in bed with all my favorite stuffies. The overhead light is off, but the room is lit by the purple and white fairy lights I bought online.

"Dr. Matthias just came by. Said you left this behind." She enters with my bag. Right. In my rush to escape, I left it on the patient bed. I'd realized it as soon as I got outside but was way too mortified to go back for it, even though it had my wallet and my phone.

I figured I wouldn't need them if I faked my own death. I'd just pay for a new identity.

Now I might *actually* die of embarrassment.

"Did you go to the clinic?" Daisy asks. She has me call her Daisy, not Grandma. Says it keeps her young.

"Yes."

"Good for you. Are you feeling better?"

I nod. I actually am feeling better, just from discussing my symptoms with a sympathetic listener. I'm also grateful that Daisy was here to answer the door for Dr. Hunk. I can't face him, but I find myself bracing for Daisy's barrage of questions.

To my surprise, she lets out a relieved sigh but doesn't pry further. "Is it okay if I head out for a bit? I'm off to check in with Old Man Duncan. He says he's noticed a strange man hanging around his house."

"What?"

"Don't you worry yourself. He's probably making it up. He wants to set up a neighborhood watch. I'll only be a half an hour." She waves a hand.

I can't believe I'm getting off so easily. Normally, Daisy pokes into every boring detail of my life. She even arranged my prom date. "I'll be fine."

"That's my girl. I'm making tortilla soup for dinner. I even got avocados to have on the side. You just rest up." She shuts the door behind her, leaving me alone.

I dig into my backpack and notice a brown bag that wasn't there before. Inside is a bottle of prescription pills—birth control and pain pills. The instructions on how to take them are written in Dr. Hunk's strong script.

Stop calling him Dr. Hunk!

The birth control pills will help even out your cycle. The pain pills are for when you're in pain.

I take one immediately with a gulp from my water bottle.

My bag holds my journal and my phone. I have a few texts from Missy, but there's another text from a contact I've never seen before. It reads only "Matthias."

What? Oh...oh wow.

Butterflies fill my belly. He entered his number into my phone. And he texted me:

> You have an appointment with Nancy tomorrow at ten am. I told Daisy you're to take the day off and rest. The painkillers will help, and Nancy will update your chart with your symptoms. PCOS is manageable with birth control.

> Set an alarm on your phone to remind yourself to take the pill at the same time every day, so you don't miss a day.

> Rest now. I mean it.

I can hear his deep voice giving me the command. My pussy clenches. Goosebumps spread all over me. God, that's hot.

Good girl, he said. And I almost came right then and there.

While I hold the phone, it starts ringing with an unknown number.

It's my dad, blowing up my phone. I made the mistake

of answering him and had to listen to his drunken ramble for fifteen minutes before I finally gave up and hung up on him.

My phone buzzes with a voicemail. I shouldn't listen to it, but I press play.

"Flower girl," my dad slurs. "I miss you. I want to see you. How 'bout you come visit me for your birthday? I'll buy you a ticket, and we can hang. It'll be like old times..." The message rambles on and on. He sounds like a loving father, except he's probably drunk. My birthday is on Valentine's day, and I wanted it to be special. I don't want to spend days traveling by bus, only to have him take me to a dingy, smoke filled casino, talk me into buying him drinks, and forget about me as soon as he's had a few.

I need to set a boundary with him, but the little girl inside me who'd do anything for her father's attention just wants to call him back, apologize, and promise to visit him. I wish I could just cut ties with him.

I don't have the energy to even think about this right now.

Baby steps.

I'll figure it out later when I'm feeling better.

I pull out my New Year's resolution list and cross off the second item. *See the doctor about PCOS.* I did it, and it feels good.

You did a brave thing coming in today, Dr. Stark said. Almost as if he knew I needed the praise.

It might be my imagination, but the bag handle holds the scent of his subtle cologne. I inhale it and imagine him saying *Good girl,* and it gives me the strength to do what I need to do next.

I pull out my phone and change his name to Dr. Stark. Then I text him,

. . .

Thank you.

I use punctuation and everything. I don't gush over him or ghost him; I just send one text. Like a normal person.

Then, I collapse back on my frilly bedspread with my hands over my face.

I've got to get my crush under control.

Chapter Three

Maisy

"They said it couldn't be done. They said we'd be under six inches of snow. But look at us now!" my grandma crows.

"Uh, Daisy?" I look up from my clipboard and look around. "We *are* under six inches of snow."

There's nothing Bad Bear Mountain loves like a festival. But this is the first annual Winterfest–a two-week event meant to bring the community together, and I'm not sure if the turnout is what we'd like.

But the cold isn't as bad as I thought it'd be. I'm in a cute GoddessWear snow outfit, cornflower blue with a faux fur hood. Daisy is in a similar ski outfit that's canary yellow. She even has her signature faux daisy fixed to her snow hat. The bright color actually looks great against her white hair.

"Nonsense. It's only three. And I told everyone to bundle up!" She bends down, scoops up a bit of snow, and packs it into a tiny snow pellet she then launches at Old Man Luther's back. "Bullseye, yeah!"

"Dagnabbit!" He claps a hand to the back of his neck as

he turns and glowers at Daisy. My grandma waves and zooms off before he gets the courage to yell at her.

I trot to keep up with her.

"What's going on with the Ferris wheel?" she asks. "Why isn't it running?"

I sigh and consult my clipboard. I found the town a killer deal on the Ferris wheel because it's off-season. No one else in New Mexico thinks it's a good idea to have an outdoor county fair in January. I wonder why?

"Maintenance check. The attendant seemed over-whelmed, so I asked Axel to help." Axel is another one of Dr. Hunk's brothers. He's amazing with anything mechanical.

"Axel, eh?" Daisy gives me a sly look. "How is that handsome young man?"

"He's a great friend," I say firmly. Daisy has tried to set me up with Axel before. She even made him be my date to senior prom. I was mortified that she asked him, but he showed up in a '69 Camaro that he'd just rebuilt from the wheels up and acted like the perfect gentleman all night.

After that, we've hung out a few times, mostly going for rides in the cars or bikes he's fixing up. He even took me to some of his races. He's a few years older than I am and effortlessly cool with his long hair, tattoo sleeves, and chill vibe. I wish I could have a crush on him.

But no, it's always been Dr. Hunk. In every romance novel I've read since I first discovered the genre at age fifteen, I've replaced the hero with Dr. Hunk. He's the man who's starred in every fantasy I've ever had.

Not Dr. Hunk. Dr. Stark. Dr. Stark. With my luck, I'll slip and call him that, and then I'll really have to change my name and move to Alaska. Or maybe somewhere warm–Mexico.

"I should get back to the Daisy Day booth before things get too busy," I say.

"No, dear. Everest has that well in hand. Or paw."

We both turn to the booth where a giant polar bear is carefully ladling out hot chocolate from a big black cauldron. The fact that there are werebears on this mountain is kind of an open secret to the two hundred citizens of Bad Bear, so the townspeople are used to the sight of Everest in bear form. Right now, the kids in line look like their every dream has come true. I get that having a polar bear serve you hot chocolate is a big attraction, but he keeps eating the marshmallows. "I guess."

"You're young." Daisy claps my shoulder. "You should be out with your friends, having fun. I know, you can ride the Ferris wheel once it's working again." She grabs my arm, and my clipboard goes flying. She tugs me towards the Ferris wheel, surprisingly strong for her age. Lately she's been weightlifting as part of Dr. Hunk...*Stark*'s health plan for her.

I look around for Missy in the crowd as she leads me over, hoping to make an excuse that will leave Daisy satisfied that I'm socializing. I really don't want to ride the Ferris wheel, not in freezing temperatures. I mean, I'm not ten years old. I especially don't need to ride it by myself. That would be...awkward. Then again, maybe Daisy needs me to get on and ride to get the party going and prove her point that it's not too cold for a Winterfest.

Yes, that probably is the case. Okay, fine. I surrender. For Daisy, I'll ride the damn thing. Even if I have to do it by myself. As Daisy's granddaughter, I am also a de facto social coordinator and representative of this town's government.

Except...oh God.

Is that Dr. Hunk standing by the Ferris wheel, talking to his brother Teddy and his brother's partner Lana?

Of course it is. There aren't that many six foot five black men on Bad Bear Mountain.

I've managed to avoid him since that embarrassing appointment a few weeks ago. I'm on birth control now, and Nancy, the nurse practitioner, is monitoring my symptoms. There isn't a cure for PCOS, but the pain medication helped me get past the ovulation pain. I'm feeling much, much better.

My other New Year's resolutions are going great, too. Missy talked me into dyeing my hair blonde, and in the spring, we both plan on walking a 5k.

That only leaves setting a boundary with my father and then...EEP...asking someone out on a date.

Unfortunately, the only man I want to be alone with is Dr. Hunk. I've been fantasizing about him for far too long in private and avoiding him in public as much as possible. It's hard to do in a town of two hundred people, but I'm committed. I've managed to never be alone with him until the disastrous day at the clinic. We exchanged two texts, and I've not seen him since.

That streak is about to end. I suck in a sharp breath and try to veer away, but Daisy has my arm. She's already lifted her hand, waving at them like she's trying to flag down a taxi.

Shit, shit, shit.

I really want to turn and run.

Where is Missy? I scan the crowd, hoping to find my bubbly friend. I need her right now. She's great at smoothing awkward conversations and filling weird silences. That's probably why she's been my best friend since I moved to Bad Bear Mountain.

It's too late. Dr. Hunk waves back at Daisy, but his gaze is on me. My breath catches under my ribs. A hot flush rushes down my arms as the memory of how it felt to be held by him teases me.

Lana and Teddy look over and wave as well. Lana's wearing a fitted gray dress that showcases her big pregnant belly. She rests her hand on her belly, and Teddy has his over hers. They are the cutest couple ever, and I swear I can feel cramping in my ovaries, like I just dropped another egg. What would it be like to have triplets with a bear-man? With Dr. Hunk...Stark...Matthias?

Whoa. My thoughts are skidding off track. I'm staring at the object of my fantasies, and it's derailing my brain.

It seems there's no escaping. I'll have to talk to him. To *them*, I mean. I'll have to talk to them.

It's not like it's a date. It's just a quick conversation before I get on the Ferris wheel. I can do this without slipping and falling into his arms, dropping something, or blurting out something stupid.

I can converse with him without sighing and fanning my face like a love-struck goon.

He's just a man. Just a gorgeous, hot, swoony doctor-man who makes my knees weak and occupies my every fantasy.

I finally manage to exhale.

Yep. I've got this.

* * *

Matthias

My gaze locks on Maisy. Even though she should be too far away for my bear to scent, the aroma of caramel and cinnamon fills my nostrils. I've been ghost-smelling her ever since Maisy visited me earlier this month.

"Dr. Matthias! There you are!" Daisy strides up to us, Maisy in tow.

Maisy's cheeks are flushed from the cold. Her blue eyes look bright against the pink of her skin.

I devour her with my stare, memorizing and documenting every detail of the way she looks right now. Her new blonde highlights frame that heart-shaped face and cherubic cheeks. The snowy mountain woods make a majestic background behind her. I freeze the image in my mind to replay tonight when my cock is in my fist.

Control.

I need to get it under control. Good thing I took a dose of Moon Cure before I came today.

"Looks like you planned a perfect Winterfest, Daisy," I say when they arrive, tearing my gaze from my beautiful mate's face.

Maisy avoids my gaze; instead, she goes straight to Lana to say hello.

"This is the first *annual* Winterfest," Daisy declares. "I'm going to make it a Bad Bear Mountain tradition."

"Bad Bear loves a good party," my brother, Teddy, observes. He's got his hand on his mate's pregnant belly. In a few months, she's giving birth to triplets.

Another set of triplet bears on Bad Bear Mountain–fate help us all.

I barely survived helping raise Bern, Hutch, and Canyon. My parents died in a car crash when I was young, and Winnie adopted me, then later, the twins, Everest and Axel, and, finally, the triplets. Shifters have super healing capacities and are normally immune to injury or disease, so my parents' deaths left me on edge. Afraid to lose my new family. I ended up studying medicine as a way to control any potential circumstances.

Maybe it wasn't fear but Fate that drove me to become a doctor because Winnie ended up with a rare shifter illness, which I was able to catch and diagnose early. I've managed to completely hide it from my brothers, inducing her into hibernation while I worked on a cure.

That left the responsibility of raising three wild teen bears mainly on me as the oldest. Not that the twins didn't pitch in when they were in town.

"I'm all about a good party," Lana agrees. "I say we come up with an excuse for one every month. It will build community."

"Yes, when are we celebrating your 90th?" I ask Daisy. She thinks I don't know she's been 89 for at least three years.

"Don't get ahead of yourself, Doctor Matthias Stark." She wags a finger. I've got a foot and a half of height on her plus a medical degree under my belt, but I feel like I'm eight years old. "Or I'll nominate you for King of Bad Bear."

"King of Bad Bear?" Lana asks, her eyes twinkling.

"I'd vote for you," Teddy grins. I shake my head at him slightly, but Daisy's already running with it.

"You should!" she cries. "Put your votes in at the Daisy Day Cafe booth. Winners will be crowned King and Queen of Bad Bear at the end of Winterfest." She points to a small stage set between two bear-shaped ice sculptures.

"How many votes per person?" Teddy asks. I can see he's plotting something.

"You can vote once a day, every day you attend Winterfest," Maisy says. My bear perks up at the sound of her soft voice. "Entries must be made in person."

"And you're welcome to campaign for your nominee," Daisy adds.

"Excellent," Teddy rubs his hands together.

"Don't," I warn, but he just chuckles. I bet he's going to recruit all of my brothers to spam the voting box and make me king. They'll get a picture of me standing on that dais in a dinky crown, holding a scepter, and then the triplets will hack professional networking accounts and post it as my profile picture.

I'm about to order Teddy not to get near the voting station when I notice my brother Axel walking towards us. He's in his signature blue jeans and black leather jacket, with his long black hair tied back out of his face like he's been working. He's also got his red metal toolbox and a wrench in hand.

"Maintenance check's done," he calls, and I notice he's looking at Maisy. "Ferris Wheel's good to go."

She smiles at him, and her whole face lights up. "Thanks, Axel."

He gives her a nod.

My hands clench into fists. Heat flares through me, red hot energy making my body ready to rage.

Against my own brother.

Maisy and Axel's whole interaction was less than ten seconds, but it was enough to tell me she's comfortable with him. More comfortable than she's ever been with me. Axel's already walking off, but I want to go after him and pulverize his face. Make sure Maisy only smiles at me.

The jealousy doesn't feel good. Axel is my most chill brother. If I talked to him, told him Maisy was my mate, he'd back off.

But no, I can't do that. Just like I can't tell my brothers about Mom. I don't burden others with the curveballs Fate throws when I can handle them on my own. That's how I maintain control.

And right now, I just need to get my emotions under control.

"All right, you kids need to help me get this party started by hopping on the Ferris wheel." Daisy hooks her arm through mine. She still has hold of poor Maisy's arm. "You two, climb on first for me." She propels us up to the wheel, cutting past the group of children and their parents who have been waiting for the ride to start. "Show everyone how safe this is."

My bear nearly roars his approval with the plan. My first instinct is to shout, YES.

Then logic kicks in. My brain calculates whether I took enough Moon Cure to be shoulder to shoulder with Maisy for an extended period.

It's probably fine.

Avoiding it would probably cause more strain on my condition because my bear would go rabid. And I need to be close to her, to cover her with my scent, so that Axel backs off.

I hold out my hand like a gentleman for Maisy when Daisy tells the attendant to start loading up, with the two of us going first.

Maisy stares at my proffered palm in surprise. Her mittened fingers lift, then freeze mid-air, like she's afraid she made a mistake.

I give her an encouraging smile. "My lady." I bow, since I look more like I'm asking her to dance at an old-fashioned ball than a guy who's about to climb on a Ferris wheel. "Shall we take a spin?"

Her cheeks flush even pinker. "Oh. Um, yes. Okay." She puts her hand in my palm, and I escort her up to the first chair. I want to pick her up by the waist and set her on the seat. To take care of her like she's mine, but I can't.

She's not mine.

She can't be mine.

I settle for sitting beside her, feeling the warmth of her small, soft body pressed next to mine. The Ferris wheel advances, loading the next passengers.

"Thank you for the prescription, I'm feeling much better," Maisy blurts.

"Of course. Anything you need, Maisy–day or night. Just text me. You have my number now."

"Oh. Um. That's very generous of you, Dr. Hu... *uhhhh*...Stark."

I've noticed Maisy always calls me Dr. Stark, even though I'm known as Dr. Matthias on the mountain. "Call me Matthias." I make it an order.

She inhales sharply, and her scent blooms stronger. "Dr...Matthias."

"Just Matthias."

Or *sir*.

"Matthias," she almost whispers.

Good girl.

I swear I feel her body heating through the contact of our thighs touching. The urge to touch her is so strong, I have to lean over the edge away from her, pretending I'm looking down.

My brother Teddy still loiters below, staring up at me like he's puzzling something out.

Fuck. Did I show my bear? Did my eyes change color when I settled beside Maisy? I've made it years without my family knowing my secret. I've always maintained my privacy with them, and with this matter, it's no different. I don't want them to worry about me going moon mad or to pressure me into claiming Maisy while she's still in her formative years.

The Ferris wheel attendant finally finishes loading everyone, and we continue rising in a gentle arc through the air.

Maisy clutches her mittened hands together in her lap and looks out at the view of our quaint little mountain town. The snow falls in steady, soft flakes, blanketing everything and making it look like a gingerbread village. "It's, um, beautiful, isn't it?"

My chest constricts. It's so precious how nervous she gets with me. My lovely mate may be human, but she feels the biological pull to me. Some part of her knows she belongs to me. Her body responds to mine. I've known she was mine since she was just fifteen—she was a late bloomer as far as puberty went.

If I didn't have my mom's illness and helping with the triplets to contend with, I would've quit my job and moved as far away from Bad Bear Mountain as I could have that very day. But I couldn't leave. And I couldn't claim her. So, I vowed never to touch her and came up with the Moon Cure.

The next time we sweep up to the top, the Ferris wheel lurches to an abrupt stop.

"What's happening?" Someone beneath us asks.

"Just a little technical difficulties, everyone!" the attendant calls out. "We'll have you back up and running in a few minutes—not to worry!"

I lean forward to peer down and see Daisy slipping him some money.

Aha! She planned this on purpose.

Maisy grips the bar in front of us. "I knew we shouldn't have gotten this thing. Even with a ninety percent discount," she mutters then winces when the car starts swinging in the cold wind. "What do you think is going on?"

I can't stop myself from putting an arm around her. "It's okay, beautiful. We're perfectly safe."

Beautiful?

Shit. Did I say that out loud?

Maisy turns her gorgeous face to mine, her blue eyes wide. She's not breathing.

The urge to kiss her overcomes me.

I don't act on it—of course I don't—but my dick thickens, and a scratchy, feverish sensation travels across my skin.

Pain seizes my lower belly, simultaneously traveling down to my balls and up to my heart.

Fuck, I want to kiss her.

Those soft, pillowy lips were *made* to be claimed by me.

My vision changes to dichromatic. I'm looking through my bear's eyes, seeing fewer colors. I blink rapidly, trying to force my bear back down. The physical pain increases. I'm not sure if it's a side effect of the Moon Cure or simply how it feels to be close to my mate without claiming her.

"Are you okay?" Maisy asks.

My grunt sounds affirmative but barely human.

She rests a soft hand on mine. Her mittens are thin, and I feel the chill of her fingers beneath them.

"You're cold," I murmur. My bear settles as I focus on her comfort. Shifters have a slightly elevated temperature, and I'm grateful for it. With my arm around her, I will my warmth to seep into her.

As soon as I'm on the ground, I'm going to tell Daisy that a Ferris wheel in January is a bad idea. The health of my patient—my most important patient—is at stake.

I hear her pulse speeding up, but she lets me cover her

mittened hands with mine. I'm so much bigger than her, and right now that's a good thing—my warmth heats us both.

"How do snowmen pay their bills?" she asks, her voice a bit breathless in a way that makes my cock perk up.

It takes me a second to realize she's telling a joke and remember how to play along. "How?"

"With cold hard cash."

A chuckle rumbles deep in my belly. I knew the punchline would be silly, but it's still funny.

"You like jokes." I'm charmed by her. She's utterly adorable.

She blushes. "I used to be afraid of everything. But I had this joke book I was obsessed with. And whenever I was scared or sad, I'd tell myself jokes over and over. And it worked. It still works." Even as she says this, her eyes dart down to the ground, and she gulps. Being stuck up here is scary for her. And cold.

I love that she's opening up to me. I rack my brain for any dad joke I know. I vow to learn a hundred by the next time I see her. The only one I can think of is painfully bad, but for her, I'll tell it. I'll do anything. "What do you call a cow with no legs?"

"What?"

"Ground beef."

Her smile lights her face.

"The triplets also had a joke book," I tell her. "They went through a period where they told the same ones over and over."

"What do you call cheese that's not yours?" she asks cheerfully. Her enthusiasm for the joke is really selling it.

I shake my head, my grin stretching my face as I wait for the punchline.

"Nacho cheese," she cries, and I crack up. My laugh creaks out of me. How long has it been since I've had a good belly laugh? Too long.

I need to laugh more. My sense of humor has gotten dusty.

I'm writing myself a prescription for more Maisy.

"You're a delight," I tell her with real feeling. She beams at me, and I'm struck by the dazzling stars in her eyes. I knew Maisy was gorgeous and just my type. But I've never gotten close enough to have a conversation with her, and now I'm regretting it. I've missed so much.

"Thank you." Her cheeks are bright. She glances down at the ground. "I hope Daisy is calling Axel back. He can fix anything."

Just like that, my jealousy is back.

"How well do you know my brother?" A growl creeps into my voice no matter how hard I try to keep it out.

"Axel? We're friends. Just friends," she clarifies with a little laugh.

I appreciate it because it allows me to get myself under control. It's not right that I want to kill my own brother just because he smiled at her.

How close are they? I've never smelled his scent on her, but I wouldn't because I've been keeping my distance from Maisy.

"He took me to prom as a favor to Daisy. Which was actually cool because everyone in my class had a crush on him." Another little laugh, this one self-deprecating. I try to keep my cool and listen, really listen.

"He takes me on rides sometimes," she sounds wistful. "We just cruise the mountain roads and listen to music. Not often, just when I need to get away from it all."

I frown. What does she need to get away from? I don't know her, not really. And I hate that.

There's a long moment of silence while she stares into the distance, and I try to read her. She's tense, almost like she's gearing up for something.

"Do you want to go on a date with me?" Maisy blurts.

I'm not sure who is more shocked—me or her. Her eyes widen even further, and she leans her head back a little, as if to create more distance between us.

I'm about to shut her down as gently as I can because there's no way on Earth I can go on a date with this exquisite creature without her ending up naked and fucked so thoroughly she wouldn't be able to walk straight when I remember her New Year's resolution list. Number six: Go on a date.

If I don't take her out, she might ask Axel or some other asshole, and I'm not sure my bear could handle that without tearing the guy to bits and scattering his body across the mountain.

Maybe it's time to stop watching her from a distance and be a bigger part of her life. I can't claim her yet, but maybe I can be the guy to help her gain some confidence.

That will mean getting closer, but I think I can manage it. I can tweak the Moon Cure compound and up my dose. That will allow me to keep my bear—and fate—under control while I help my beautiful girl spread her wings and fly.

Maybe it's time for me to break my rules.

Time for me to recognize my interest in Maisy for what it is...

She's my fated mate.

She belongs to me, which means she's mine to encourage and mold. If I'm careful, I might be able to do that without taking over her life. I can be the Mr. Knightly to her Emma–guiding and encouraging until she's matured enough to handle a man like me.

Besides, I don't think I can stay away. I need more Maisy in my life.

She reads my hesitation as rejection, and her face turns a deep shade of purple. "Sorry," she says. "That was highly inappropriate. I mean, you're my doctor and all..."

I'm not her main medical care provider, actually, but I realize she's trying to give me an out.

I take her hand again. "I would love to go on a date with you, Maisy."

Chapter Four

M*aisy*

I can't believe I actually did it. I asked my crush on a date. And he said yes!

I never could've done it, but being with him is so...easy. I feel so relaxed.

Except now that I've done it, I realize what I've done.

"You would?" Inexplicably, my eyes fill with tears, and I blink them back. Why in the hell would I feel like crying when the man I've been fantasizing about since I was a teen said he'd like to go on a date with me?

It doesn't even make sense, but I often feel that way about my body. "Really?"

"Of course." He's still holding my hand, and I realize I'm squeezing the shit out of it.

I release him with a squeak.

I'm suddenly beyond embarrassed. Too much emotion–emotion I don't even understand–floods me. Waves of excitement, heat, and power seem to cook me in their juices. It's too much. I look over the side of the Ferris wheel. Would it be possible to launch myself right off the side?

Matthias corrals me closer with an arm around my shoulders, as if he guesses at my intention to flee. He's so warm, I want to burrow into him like he's a big blanket and never leave.

"Dinner?" he suggests.

Panic eclipses all my other emotions. "Uhh." I'm imagining myself at a restaurant with him, trying to make conversation while not spilling anything on myself.

"Or a hike."

Relief floods me. I can handle a hike. It'll be chill and private. I want to go to a candlelit dinner, but I'm not sure I'm ready for it.

It feels safer to go off somewhere private.

And it'll mean we won't have the town gossiping about us.

Maybe it'll be better for him not to be seen with me. It's possible this sort of date keeps us in the friend-zone.

But that's okay.

That's totally fine.

The point is, I dared to ask my long-time crush on a date, and he accepted.

I can cross off one of my New Year's resolutions. It doesn't matter how the actual date goes. Baby steps. I'm moving forward toward becoming the person I want to become.

This year, I'm determined to crawl out of the shadows of my charismatic grandmother and gorgeous best friend. I may not be ready to shout to the world about my future plans but... baby steps.

"Sure. A hike sounds great. Just us...alone." I press my lips together to keep from rambling. I don't want him to think I want to get him alone to...do stuff. Just because I fantasize about ripping his clothes off doesn't mean I'm going to do it.

Matthias studies my face, which makes me want to throw myself over the side of the ride again.

My phone rings in my purse. Saved by the bell.

I pull out my phone, but when I see the number I send it to voicemail. A few seconds later, the phone starts ringing again. I send it to voicemail again.

"Are you dodging someone's calls?" Matthias's smooth brow furrows.

The familiar sick feeling I get every time I see my dad's number pop up swirls in my belly. Like grease in mud water.

"Oh, uh, no. I mean, it's nothing. Not important. I'm not taking it."

"Who is it?" Matthias' voice suddenly takes on that authoritative ring that makes me turn to mush. The tone he used on me in the clinic.

I'm going to need to hear a yes, Matthias.

To which my body answers: *Yes, Matthias. God, yes!*

"Uh..." I freeze. My parents are a source of great shame. Daisy doesn't like me to talk about them. She was able to keep my dad from only seeing me on supervised visits until I was eighteen, but now he can reach out directly to me, and I'm torn.

"Is someone bothering you, Maisy?" The deep, protective timbre of Matthias' voice makes me swoon.

"It's, um..." I realize I don't owe him any information, even if he is the object of my crush. So I grow a backbone and say, "It's personal."

Daisy would appreciate that answer. She doesn't want people to know there's something sordid in her family. Of course, she still grieves my mom's tragic foray into drug addiction that eventually led to her death. I would say I do, too, but honestly, coming to Bad Bear Mountain to live with Daisy at age five was the best thing that happened to me, so I guess I believe everything happened for a reason.

Matthias nods. "Of course. I didn't mean to intrude." His gaze lingers on me, like despite his soothing words, he's still waiting for an answer.

I swallow. "My dad usually reaches out when he wants money," I admit. "He says he wants me to visit him for my birthday next month, but it's probably a lie just to get me talking to him again. So I've been dodging his calls."

Matthias' face darkens, but he doesn't look shocked. It's almost like he already knew I had a deadbeat dad. Or it doesn't faze him.

"And you don't want to block him because he's your dad," he fills in.

I nod miserably.

"Oh, beautiful." Matthias' arm is still around the back of the seat, and he uses it to give me a side hug.

Every time he calls me *beautiful*, my pussy clenches, and my panties grow damp.

I mean, it must mean something, right?

It can't be something he calls all his patients. Or even all the women in his life. I mean...*beautiful?* It's an endearment.

And God, do I want to be his dear one. The thought practically makes me dizzy.

"That's hard."

His sympathy chokes me up. Because my parents are a topic I can't discuss with anyone–not even with Missy– getting it out and having someone else greet the news with compassion makes tears burn behind my eyes.

"It's okay," I say. "I have no expectations of him at all."

44

"What does Daisy say about it?"

"I can't tell her." I sigh. "She gets upset about the way he manipulates me."

"So you're carrying this alone."

"Yeah."

Matthias holds out his hand. "Give me your phone."

I hand it to him before I realize what I'm doing. It's so easy to follow his orders.

He pulls up my dad's number. I haven't saved it, probably because I don't want to see his name. I don't want him in my life.

Matthias holds my gaze with his dark brown eyes as he presses the button to block the number.

Suddenly, I feel a hundred pounds lighter. I sigh, feeling my tense shoulders relax. "Thank you."

"Anytime." He further unnerves me by leaning over and kissing the top of my head.

Is that...a fatherly kiss? Or something different?

A child below us starts crying, frightened by the stopped ride, and the Ferris wheel suddenly lurches back into motion. It's almost as if the attendant was just waiting for someone to really complain. Or as if it had been stopped on purpose.

Wait...Oh God. Daisy probably arranged for this to happen!

I love my grandma dearly, but she is way too up in my business.

"Oh good. We're not stranded," I say to fill space. To change the topic from my dad.

"Yes." Matthias sits back in his seat and, tragically, withdraws his arm from around me.

Awkward.

I inhale his scent. It's wild and woodsy with a sophisticated edge of expensive cologne. I hope the scent lingers on my clothes.

As soon as our Ferris wheel car reaches the platform, I'm clambering out of the seat. The car rocks a little, and Matthias takes my arm to steady me.

"Easy, beautiful." He ends up helping me out. His big hand rests on my back, and I sigh with how right it feels.

"Thanks," I murmur. Luckily, Daisy has made herself scarce. I don't want her here grilling Matthias and me on our ride together. She's been better about getting involved in my business, but today proves she's not above contriving situations to make sure I'm alone with my crush.

"Anytime." Matthias brushes a strand of hair back from my cheek. "When did you change your hair?"

"Um, last week. Missy helped me dye it."

"It looks beautiful." His eyes crinkle at me as he smiles, and it's like the sun is shining on me.

"Maisy!" A cheery voice calls, but I can't drag my eyes away from Matthias until my best friend runs up to me.

"Dr. Matthias, hey." Missy tosses her blonde hair over her shoulder. She doesn't try to flirt, but she doesn't need to try. She's effortlessly gorgeous, and years of theater and beauty pageant training means she's always unconsciously posing for an audience.

"Hello, Missy," Matthias greets her. I try not to notice how good they look together. The two most beautiful people on Bad Bear Mountain. "I didn't know you were back in town."

"I came back for the holidays." Missy beams. "Hollywood is amazing, but it's so nice to be home." She flutters her long eyelashes, as if inviting him to ask about her budding actress career.

"There's no place like Bad Bear," Matthias says then

switches his attention to gaze down at me. "What did the wave say to the shore?"

It takes me a second to realize he's telling another dad joke.

"*Sea* you later." His deep voice makes the silly joke the sexiest thing I've ever heard. I feel like I have a fever, except it feels good.

He's reminding me of our date.

"Yes, Matthias." I use his name as instructed. "Text me the details?"

"I will." His eyes flash with a blue light, and he dips his head towards me. "'Til then, Maisy." With a nod to Missy, he leaves.

"Bye," I whisper, feeling warm and happy inside, like I just drank the best hot chocolate. I can't believe I have an inside joke with Dr. Matthias.

"Oh my goddess," Missy turns to me with her eyes wide. "Did you just have a moment with Dr. Matthias?" Her voice is so loud, I feel like everyone can hear.

"Shhh." I wrap my arm around her and hustle her away to find some privacy. She'll want to know what just happened, and I need to verbally process. "I'll tell you everything. Just not in the middle of town."

"You better," Missy says, and I can't help giggling.

I have a date. With Matthias! For once, everything is going my way.

* * *

Matthias

I'm going on a date with Maisy. My *mate*.

I am so fucked.

I've also never been happier.

peRenee Rose & Lee Savino

After I left Winterfest, I texted her to set the date for tomorrow. Sundays the cafe closes early, so she'll be free. At three pm, we'll meet at the head of Bad Bear Trail and hike to the overlook.

My bear is so excited, I had to let him out and do laps around the mountain to use up some of the excess energy. I ended up chopping enough wood to fire my wood stove for the next three winters. I hauled some to Ma's, too. My bear wanted me to drop off a cord at Daisy's house, but I knew that would lead to him snooping in Maisy's window. She's never seen my bear yet, and I don't want to scare her.

Instead, I settle into my cabin for a rare night off. After a dinner of braised short ribs, mashed cauliflower, and about a pound of sauteed kale, I pour myself a cup of dandelion tea. I'm about to relax into my favorite armchair by the roaring fire when there's a hard knock on the door. Before I can shout "Go away," my brothers burst into my space.

Not just Teddy but Darius, too. And Axel. At least they didn't bring Everest and the triplets. There's not enough room for all of us in here, especially since Everest insists on remaining in bear form.

A blast of cold wind follows my brothers in.

"Shut the door," I bark. Axel slams it behind him.

"Now leave and then shut it," I mutter, but I don't use alpha command to make it an order.

Darius holds up a bottle of whiskey.

"Fine." I wave them in. Axel sits in front of the hearth. Teddy and Darius sit on my couch, which creaks under their muscled bulk.

"Don't break my couch." I point at them. They have a habit of fighting each other whenever they get within arm's distance, and the couch is barely big enough to hold both of them.

"No fighting," they say in unison, holding their hands up in an identical movement. They're even dressed similarly, Teddy in a blue plaid shirt with a little brown bear embroidered on the pocket and Darius in a matching green one. Both of them are wearing jeans–and the same brown boots.

"Did you guys dress to match on purpose?" I ask. "Or are your mates conspiring to make you look like twinsies?"

Teddy and Darius glance at each other and then do a double take. Their faces take on identical outraged expressions. Axel laughs.

I take a sip of tea to hide my smirk.

"My mate can dress me any day of the week," Darius announces.

"Mine too. Lana has excellent taste," Teddy says quickly.

"So does Paloma," Darius boasts. "And she's a billionaire, so price isn't an issue."

"Lana's a billionaire too. And an internationally recognized fashionista." Teddy glares at Darius, who glares right back.

Fates, now they're using their mates to one-up each other.

"Both of your mates are amazing," I say. "And neither of you deserve them. Now, why are you here?"

"What, we can't come hang with our big brother?" Axel lounges back beside the fire.

"No." I narrow my eyes at him. I haven't forgotten how close he is with Maisy. I need to figure out a way to get him to back off without outright staking my claim. "What's going on?"

"Two things. One, I caught some strange scents on the mountain," Darius says. "Smelled it when I was on a walk with Paloma. Two males, smokers. One has a greasy, bitter scent."

"This was up on Lilac Lane," Darius says. "Near Old Man Luther's place. And Daisy's."

My bear gets agitated at the mention of Daisy. Maisy lives with her grandmother. Neither my bear nor I like the idea of a stranger hanging around their house.

For some reason, I think of all those missed calls on Maisy's phone. She said it was her father, asking for money. Did he drive up here to pester her?

"Could be some workmen," Teddy says. "But Old Man Luther says he's seen a car hanging around with Nevada plates. They might be a visitors, but he wants to put together a neighborhood watch."

"You have your own security, right?" I ask. Lana and Paloma have both been targeted before, and we bears don't mess around when it comes to protecting what's ours.

"Black Wolf is monitoring our property," Teddy says.

"Mine and Paloma's too," Darius says.

I nod slowly. Black Wolf, the private security firm Teddy pilots helicopters for, is a shifter-owned operation located out of Taos, New Mexico. All the operatives, like Teddy, are shifters and former special ops military. In addition to their shifter strength and regenerative powers, they have the highest level of training, discipline, and the best equipment in the world. They are the best.

"But they keep their surveillance to our property," Darius adds. "House and land, of course, but it's not the whole mountain. We can get them to do a one-time sweep of all of Bad Bear. But we want to respect our neighbors' privacy. Unless it's an active threat."

"I'll check it out," I say. My bear wanted to sniff around

Maisy's home, anyway. Maybe I should've gone with the instinct.

"You're busy. Teddy and I will do it, and just in case, we'll both train the triplets to run patrols," Darius says.

I raise a skeptical brow.

"Hey, they're more responsible these days," Teddy says. "Ever since you made them do that bootcamp with Black Wolf."

"You still see them as goofy teens," Axel says. "They've matured."

"They put a whoopie cushion on everyone's chair at Christmas," I point out.

"That wasn't them," Axel says smugly.

I shake my head. I forget that Axel is only a few years older than the triplets. Just two years older than Maisy—another reason I should stay away from her.

He's quiet, and people assume he's mature, but there's a wicked prankster under his chill vibe. He gets up to more trouble than the rest of us combined. He's just better at getting away with it.

"Now that that's settled..." Darius leans forward. His bear emerges, making his eyes flash gold. "Matthias, when were you going to tell us Daisy's granddaughter is your mate?"

Chapter Five

Matthias

I stare down my brothers. My bear answers to no one.

But there's no one I'd rather talk about than Maisy. And I need to stake my claim. Axel was her prom date, once upon a time. He did it as a favor to Daisy, but just in case...I need to make sure he knows she's off limits.

"Daisy's granddaughter, huh?" Teddy raises a brow at me.

"She has a name," I say. "It's Maisy." It's actually Daisy May Bennett the Third, but she goes by Maisy. Too many people call her Daisy or Missy. They mix her up with her grandmother or her best friend, Missy.

Which isn't right. Maisy deserves a spotlight of her own.

"We're going on a date. And none of you are to interfere," I order them. Their eyes flash at me as their bears acknowledge the command.

I wait for Axel to protest, but he's wearing a small smile.

"Maisy and Matthias," Teddy says. He opens the bottle

of whiskey. "I'll drink to that." he chugs straight from the bottle. As soon as he's done, he hands it to Darius, who does the same thing.

"It's not like that. It's just a date." I can't lie to them and say Maisy isn't my mate. They'll smell that I'm lying.

But I'm not going to claim her. I'm not going to take her choices from her.

"Don't deny it, brother," Axel says. "It just makes it harder in the end."

"What do you know about it?" I shoot back. "And how do you know Maisy?"

Axel stretches lazily. "She's a friend. I always thought whoever she chooses to date would win the jackpot. She's beautiful, kind, focused, amazing..."

My growl rips out of me. I grit my teeth, and it cuts off. The intensity stunned me.

I have to get control of myself.

"She is. You're not to get near her," I say. Tension crackles in the air. Teddy and Darius exchange looks, as if planning on how they'll interfere if I jump on Axel and start whaling on him.

"I won't, brother. I've been keeping an eye on her, but if you're going to do it, I won't have to."

"You don't. I'll be watching over her from now on."

Axel just grins, cool as a cucumber, and beckons for the twins to hand him the whiskey. He chugs it, and I wrinkle my nose. Drinking from the same bottle is disgusting. A health hazard.

But the more I watch them, the more I want to take a shot. I need it to distract me from thinking about Maisy. Her soft lips, her shining hair, her excitement when she told me the stalest jokes imaginable...just to make sure I wasn't afraid.

Ours. My bear says. *Our Maisy.*

My phone flashes with a text. I look down and see it's Maisy.

She's replying to my text about our date.

> Sounds good! See you then.

Then...

> What do you call a prom in the North Pole?

> A snow ball!

I chuckle to myself. I need to get that joke book from my youngest brothers and study up, so I can keep the joke volley going.

When I look up, my three brothers are staring at me.

I tuck away my phone and clear my throat. "What?"

"You just...laughed," Teddy narrows his eyes at me.

"I laugh."

Axel snorts.

"What? I do. Shut up."

"He's going to fall and fall hard," Teddy says. "I'll bet anything."

"I'll take that bet," Darius says.

Teddy holds out a hand and Darius takes it. They both shake without looking at each other. Their eyes are fixed on me.

I briefly consider fratricide.

Not worth it. Paloma and Lana would kill me.

"You're wrong," I grumble. But when Axel passes the whiskey to me, I take a swig and let it burn down my throat.

Tomorrow I am going on a date with Maisy. And there's

not enough Moon Cure to keep me fantasizing about kissing the hell out of my lovely mate.

I am so fucked.

I can't wait.

* * *

Maisy

I'm sitting at my vanity, a makeup mirror propped on my entrepreneurship textbooks in front of me. Getting ready for my date. With Dr. Hu–Stark. *Matthias.*

Cue internal screaming.

The only thing keeping me from melting into a puddle on the floor is my determination to be early to our hike, so I don't keep him waiting.

> When's your birthday?

He texted me earlier.

> You said it's coming up.

> Valentine's day.

I want to ask why he wants to know, but before I work up the nerve to be flirty, he texts back.

> I'll have to get you a good present.

Squee!!!

I can't believe this is happening. A date with Dr. Hunk? What even is my life? At this rate, I'll be done with my New Year's list by my birthday. All my baby steps are adding up to big changes.

Even my old familiar bedroom is transformed. No more dusty participation trophies or boy band posters on the walls. I cleaned out my closet and donated all my clothes from my high school years. Goodbye baggy t-shirts and uncomfortable jeans. Now everything I reach for flatters my wide hips and big, gorgeous butt. Thanks to Lana Langmeyer and her GoddessWear, I'm learning to embrace my style.

And my room no longer feels like a child's. It doesn't remind me of the person I used to be.

Now I just need to upgrade my makeup look. Missy was supposed to come over and help, but her mom needed her in Sante Fe for a family event, so she's talking me through it over the phone. My favorite unicorn stuffie, Mr. Sparkles, holds my phone. Because I'm a grown-ass woman, but I'll treasure my stuffies forever.

My goal is to figure out how to apply eyeliner without stabbing myself in the cornea.

"I'm just saying you would love it," Missy says. I have her on speakerphone. She was telling me how to do a cat-eye, but got side-tracked talking about her new life in L.A. She moved out there last year to make a go at her acting career, but she ran out of money and is home living with her parents in Santa Fe while she regroups. "Hollywood is so amazing."

"I know *you* love it, but I don't think it's for me. You're there to break into acting. What would I even do?"

"You work at a coffee shop. You can get a job anywhere."

Ouch.

I frown. "I'm a manager at Daisy Day. I set my own hours. I have a lot of creative control." I don't just make lattes. I do the books and plan the marketing campaigns.

Daisy is busy with being mayor and all her side projects. The cafe's success is something I'm proud of, something I intend to build off.

A big move to the West Coast would be fun. But I've already made big changes–they might seem small to the outside world, but they were big for me. My self-esteem has grown by leaps and bounds.

I've been wearing crop tops more often, too, and I look cute!

I have big, big plans, but they're still in the incubator. I haven't shared them with anyone. So all I say is, "I love Bad Bear. I don't want to leave."

"I know you love Bad Bear, but do you ever want something more?"

I do, actually. I want to expand the cafe–that's why I'm taking small business classes to study the best way to do it. I'm tempted to tell this to Missy, but I imagine her wrinkling her nose in disbelief and asking why I would even attempt something like this. All she sees is me pulling espresso shots. That's all anyone sees. And I'm fine with it.

"In Hollywood, we could live together. It'd be so much fun."

Hmm, up until now I've been flattered that she's inviting me to go with her, but maybe she just needs someone to help her pay rent.

"I'm sure you can find an awesome roommate," I say gently. "Maybe someone who's trying to be an actress too."

"I'm not *trying* to be an actress," Missy snips. "I *am* one. I've been in three commercials."

For her dad's Santa Fe dealership. When she was sixteen. I know her dreams are bigger, but it seems she hasn't had much success in Hollywood. She hasn't shared this with me, but I can tell. Her usually bubbly enthusiasm is fraying at the seams. She doesn't want her peak to be winning Miss New Mexico Teen at age fourteen.

She sighs. "Sorry I snapped at you. It's just...everyone there is so cutthroat. If I roomed with another aspiring actress, I'd be afraid she'd shave off my hair in my sleep. Something to sabotage me."

I wince. "That's awful."

"I'm all alone out there. You're my best friend; you've always been there for me."

"That's what friends do. But I have my own life." I put down the eyeliner. I'll save the make-up lesson for another time.

"I'm sorry," she says again. "I'm supposed to be helping you get ready for your date."

"It's okay."

"I'll make it up to you. But honestly, Maisy, you don't really need my help," she says. "You're beautiful without any makeup, you always have been. Your skin is perfect." She sounds wistful, almost envious, but that's ridiculous. Missy is a literal beauty queen. Why would she be jealous of me?

She was such a good, loyal friend in high school, even though I felt like a side character in her glamorous life.

Her mom shouts her name, and she winces. "I have to go. But I'm counting down the hours until I can call you again. I want to hear all about your date." She wishes me luck, and we say goodbye.

My date. I shove down the fluttering butterflies in my stomach.

Guess I'm on my own. But...I have my own back. That's what the last few weeks have taught me. And Matthias said yes to a date when I was wearing minimal make-up. We're going on a hike, it's not like I need to go full glam.

I pick up my favorite peachy blush with new determination.

What kind of father buys his daughter makeup?

A MAC daddy.

Our doorbell rings, and I drop the blush with a clatter.
Is Matthias here? No, we said we'd meet at the trailhead. In
two hours.

There's a big, shadowy figure beyond the door. I hesitate, but I know everyone on Bad Bear Mountain.

But when I open it, I don't recognize the guy at all. He's
a huge white guy with a beer gut, middle-aged with a ruddy
complexion. His clothes reek of cigarette smoke.

"Maisy Bennett?" He looks me up and down.

"Who are you?"

"Your dad's been trying to reach you," he says.

A cold wind blows through me. My dad...is troubled.
He's an addict, which means he's been a shitty father. I've
had therapy, so I know it's not my fault, but it's still hard not
to want something from him—love, attention, caring—whatever, and then still be disappointed when he never gives it.

I'm glad Matthias helped me block his calls. I should've
cut him out years ago.

"He wants to talk to you," the man says.

"I don't want to talk to him."

"Not an option."

That's when I notice that there's a big white creeper
van with Nevada plates parked out by our mailbox. I've
noticed it around a few times and thought it was a
paint van.

I don't have a good feeling about this. Something tells
me to slam the door in the guy's face, so I do, but he has his
boot propping it open.

He grabs my arm, and shock makes me freeze. I open

my mouth to scream, but he pulls close and covers my mouth. His hand smells like tobacco, and I gag.

I hear the footfalls of a second pair of boots. There's another guy here, tall and thin with stringy hair around his pale and narrow face. He's holding a syringe in his hand. Terror grips me, and the world wavers as the second guy comes close to stick me with the needle.

"You're coming with us," he says.

"No," I whimper through the hand clamped over my mouth. For a wild second, I see Matthias's face in front of mine. He'll be at the trailhead waiting for me. We're supposed to go on a date.

Today was supposed to be the best day of my life.

There's a prick on my arm, and the world swirls away.

* * *

Matthias

I'm ten minutes early to our meeting point at the trail-head. My bear is antsy even though I took a dose of Moon Cure before I came. Dullness radiates through my limbs and torso, muting my hunger, blunting my fangs. I convinced my bear that taking a dose was for the best to protect Maisy, but neither of us like how it numbs us.

My bear grows more agitated five minutes past the hour, so I text her. Fifteen minutes in, my bear is so riled I have to start pacing to let some energy out.

She wouldn't be late. Or maybe she would be. I know everything is to know about Maisy on paper—from a distance. But I purposely haven't engaged with her much socially.

Is she the type to show up late? Somehow, it doesn't seem like her. She's responsible. Organized. Shy.

Thirty minutes in, I call Maisy, and when it goes to voicemail, I pocket my phone and jog toward her house.

Something's wrong.

Now I'm sure. Maisy wouldn't be late. She's a very organized person. Most people don't realize how much she does. She manages a coffee shop that's more than a place to get a drink—it's the social hub and true third space that creates community in our small town. I suspect she's the reason Daisy is so successful as mayor, too. She's the quiet competence executing Daisy's wild hare-brained schemes.

Did she change her mind about the date? Was she too intimidated to text me? I know how much I fluster her.

But no, she's too kind, and she respects me too much. She wouldn't leave me hanging.

Which means my bear is right to be upset. Fuck! I should have called her immediately.

I have a bad feeling about this.

I smell something foul as I step onto her street. *Cigarettes, strange human,* my bear reports.

I speed up to a run.

When I get to Maisy's house, the door is cracked open. I ring the bell and knock, calling her name. Maybe she just got busy with work stuff and lost track of time.

I call her again and hear her phone ringing...inside the house.

Oh, fate. I don't like this.

She's not here. As soon as I accept that, I can pay attention to what my bear is screaming at me.

There's a strong scent by the door. A hunting dog can sniff out a trail by following the cloud of skin cells and scent molecules a person leaves behind. A shifter's nose is even more sensitive.

It's a gift and a curse. And right now, it's torture because

I can smell what Maisy was feeling when the strange men confronted her on her doorstep.

Terror. Sharp and acidic, burning my nose along with the strong smell of stale cigarettes. She was here not long ago, along with at least two strange men. I trace the scent to the mailbox, where it disappears. She must've been put in a vehicle of some kind and driven away. The trail ends there. Maisy's sweet scent snuffed out by the smell of diesel and axle grease.

She's gone.

My bear roars.

Stop, I tell him, and he replies with a stream of words: *Mate Danger Kill Strangers Protect Mate.*

Later, I promise him. Right now, I need to think.

I call Daisy. We quickly figure out Maisy isn't with her, and no one has seen her since she left work.

"Meet me at your house." I try not to sound panicked.

I shoot a text to the group chat containing all my brothers.

911. Maisy's gone. Someone's taken her.

Chapter Six

Matthias

Minutes later, my brothers assemble at Daisy's. The triplets are even here, looking more serious than I've seen them.

Everest paces around in bear form, snuffling at the ground and pavement.

Axel, our car and motorcycle expert, squats by Maisy and Daisy's mailbox. It's white and decorated with hand-painted yellow daisies. On the pavement in front of it are fresh tire marks.

"They put her in a van," Axel says. "And drove that way." He starts jogging, following the tracks.

"And no one saw?" I ask.

"Go door knocking," Teddy orders The Threes in his special ops command tone. "Find anyone who saw anything."

The triplets salute and scatter.

Daisy and Darius emerge from the house.

"Her phone is still in her bedroom." Daisy hands it to me. She looks pale and shaken.

I scroll through Maisy's phone and see that there are no more calls from the unknown number. It looks like she kept it blocked.

Canyon dashes up to us. He's sweating like he sprinted up the whole mountain, but he's not breathing hard. "Old Man Luther saw a white van hanging around here two hours ago," he reports. "And Jasmine Wilkins was at the playground with her son. She told me about a 'creeper van' driving past real fast."

"They're off the mountain then." I sound wooden because it takes all my effort to hold back my bear, who is tearing to the surface.

"I've got Black Wolf online," Teddy says, holding up his phone. "They're expanding surveillance to Route Seven and the highway all the way to Santa Fe."

"It's too late. This happened at least an hour ago, maybe more." I resist the urge to lift my face to the sky and give a full bear roar. "Who took her? And where? And why?"

Daisy's legs buckle under her. Darius and Teddy are right there to catch her and ease her down.

"I can't do this," she whispers, dazedly. All her spryness is gone, and she looks like she's shrunken.

I crouch, checking her vitals as I've done for years—since before I went to med school. Daisy's been my number one patient for a long time—since she adopted Maisy and came to me and begged for help staying healthy, so she could raise her granddaughter.

She's okay, she's just in shock.

"She's alone. She might be hurt. Who would do this?" She turns wet eyes to me.

I see so much of Maisy in her.

"I don't know," I growl, no longer interested in hiding

my ferocious side. "But I'll find them. And I'll make them pay."

I stand but stay close to Daisy in case she faints.

"Wren's at Mission Control," Canyon says. I thought it was cute that they called their large TV gaming set-up at Paloma's home movie theater "Mission Control," but now it fits. "She's contacted Kylie. They're both digging into the dark web, trying to see if anyone posted a job about Bad Bear Mountain."

Kylie is a wolf shifter billionaire and genius hacker. Wren is Paloma's younger sister.

"Do you think we're the target?" Darius asks in a low voice. "Or Maisy?"

I rub the back of my neck. "They took her. But there's no way to know until we find her."

"Kylie will look into Maisy's background, too," Teddy said.

"Her father," Daisy mutters from her huddle on her front stoop. She's looking a little stronger. "He's been calling her. I bet he's behind this."

"Tell Kylie to look into Maisy's father too," I order.

"Allen. Allen Dankworth," Daisy tells us the name. "He and my Donna met in Vegas. I think he still lives there."

"He's been calling her." I hand Canyon Maisy's phone. "It's a Nevada number."

"I'll see if Hutch and Wren can get an exact location." Canyon rushes off.

"I'll tell Black Wolf to look at routes between here and Vegas," Darius says and strides off.

I stand still for a moment, feeling helpless.

"She'll be okay, brother," Teddy murmurs to me. "If it's her dad, that means she'll be alive."

"He's not a good person." Daisy's voice quavers.

"No, he's not." I've never met him, but I already know he doesn't deserve Maisy. "But Maisy is strong."

A helicopter zooms overhead with Bern at the controls. The wind whips around us as it lands in a field at the end of the street.

Daisy grabs my hand, her frail fingers turned to claws, her grip surprisingly strong.

"You bring her back, Matthias." Her voice is almost swallowed by the noise of the helicopter. "You find her and bring her back home."

"I will," I vow with every molecule of my being. Her hand goes limp in mine, like it took all her energy to grab my hand and make me promise to save Maisy. I let her go and stride towards the waiting helicopter, ripping off my glasses as I go. My eyesight is perfect; I only wear them to make me look more scholarly. It's part of my persona to get my patients to relax. I won't need them where I'm going.

I'm no longer the kind doctor of Bad Bear. I am a bad bear ready to rampage, and I'm on a mission to find my mate.

I will destroy anyone and everyone who touched her.

* * *

Maisy

There's a nail in my skull, splitting it down the middle. At least, that's what it feels like. When I move to touch it, the pain is drowned out by the aches in my entire body. My hair is a curtain over my face.

I'm lying on a bed, on top of the blankets. The only light in the room comes from the glow around the window.

My mouth feels like it's been filled with rancid cotton.

I try to sit and a wave of wooziness washes over me. I feel like I've been drugged.

Because I was.

I slide to the edge of the bed, closing my eyes when the room spins. *Baby steps.*

At least this place is small. It's nice enough for a generic hotel room, but the whole place stinks like cigarette smoke. The smell doesn't help the state of my head.

I make my way to the bathroom and gulp water then empty my screaming bladder. There are white towels neatly folded under the sink, and I wet one and use it to wipe my skin. It makes me feel a little bit better.

But I keep the lights off in case it'll summon whoever kidnapped me.

Because I *have* been kidnapped. Those two guys ambushed me at my house and committed several felonies.

I look pale in the mirror. I'm not okay.

"Don't eat a clock," I whisper to my reflection. "It's time-consuming."

My favorite joke doesn't dent my fear, but it's familiar. I'm an adult. I can get through this.

Bad jokes won't get me through this fear. When I close my eyes, all I see is Matthias. His beautiful brown eyes looking at me. Seeing me. The real me.

I missed our date. If I think about that too much, I'm going to cry.

Focus, beautiful, I imagine Matthias saying to me. *You got this. Baby steps.*

I'm still in my yoga pants and a soft sweater–the outfit I was going to wear under my coat on the hike. They're a bit worse for wear–dirty, like I've been rolling around in the back of that creeper van–but at least I have clothes. It doesn't seem like anyone has touched me, other than sticking a needle in my neck, drugging me, and dragging me to the van. Then driving me here, wherever here is.

The clock reads just after midnight. Which means I was asleep for ten hours.

I take a deep breath. First things first, I'm going to figure out where I am.

Then I'm going to figure out what I can do about it.

I'm still weak from whatever they drugged me with, so I need to move slowly.

I go to the door and try the handle, but it's locked. I fight my panic.

Instead of turning on the lights, I head to the window and pull back the curtains. And almost have a heart attack.

I'm in a room high above a nighttime cityscape. The city below is a flat grid stretching to the distant mountains. A few miles away are a bunch of glittering towers and a huge lit up dome.

Vegas.

I'm in Vegas.

What the F? Did those guys toss me in the back of a van and drive me all the way here? No wonder my whole body aches.

This has to do with my dad. He used to live in Vegas, probably still does. Somehow, this has to do with him.

That thought should comfort me, but it doesn't. Why would my dad kidnap me? I knew he ran with a bad crowd, but they're all pretty stupid. This is an elaborate scheme that requires focus. A bunch of druggies couldn't do this, could they?

And why would they do it?

I put a hand on my chest and belly and start deep breathing exercises before I have a panic attack and pass out. Whatever they used to drug me is still in my system, making me sluggish, but my heart is racing.

I look for a phone, so I can call 911. Or Matthias. For some reason, I'd rather call Matthias, which is illogical, since he's back in New Mexico, and I'm in Las Vegas, but I need a dose of his cool, calm, and collected demeanor. I need him to tell me what to do.

I find the phone jack, but the phone has been removed. Dammit! Maybe I can bang on the door and attract some attention.

I start toward it, but just then, the handle turns, and the door swings in.

I gasp, taking a step back.

Chapter Seven

Maisy

The person who just entered switches on the lights, temporarily blinding me. I shrink back toward the windows, squinting at them until my vision clears.

"Dad?"

"Hey, flower girl." My dad looks older than ever, even though he's only mid-forties. He knocked my mom up when they were young twenty-somethings working at the casinos and partying hard. His face is red, his eyes bloodshot, but he doesn't look drunk or high. He's in a white button-down shirt and faded black slacks, which is dressed up for him.

"What's going on? Why am I here?"

"What, no hug for your dear ole dad?" He opens his arms, showing the yellowed patches under his arms.

I'm speechless with an emotion I can't name. And then I realize what I'm feeling.

Rage.

"No, *Allen*," I use his name because he's not a parent to me. He never was. It's about time I made that clear. "I want to know why I'm in Vegas." I harden my voice. "You're going to tell me what's going on, right now."

Allen sighs and rubs a hand over his head, his gaze dropping to the carpet. "Yeah, this didn't go how I'd like. You should've answered your phone," he says accusingly. "I've been calling you."

"I was busy," I say. I don't say the obvious–that I blocked him because I want him out of my life. Things have escalated into terrifying territory, and I need to play this smart. I might need to charm my dad long enough to get out of here.

Because I will escape. I promise myself that.

Good girl, I imagine Matthias saying. *You've got this.*

"Just tell me what's going on."

"Aww, it's..." he mumbles and sighs. "I got myself in some trouble. I was working for a guy, and some stuff happened, and now I owe him a lot of money. He's not a good guy, Daisy." He uses my legal name.

"It's *Maisy,*" I correct him, while I scramble to figure out what he just told me. When he was sober, Allen used to get work at casinos. Not the nice ones on the strip but the old ones off strip. Now I'm pretty sure he's unhireable, except for working for criminals who are running drugs. "Let me get this straight. You owe money to someone powerful. Someone used to getting what he wants."

Allen nods, and I curl my hands into fists.

Of course, this has to do with money. Even when I was ten, the sperm donor would tell me to ask Daisy for money. Once I gave him my birthday money, but Daisy found out and was upset, so I never did that again. "So what does he want from me?" I'm a manager of a cafe, not a millionaire.

He mumbles something, looking down at the carpet like he's five and not forty-five.

"I need you to repeat that." Before he says anything, I know it's going to be bad.

"He wants to marry you."

I'm sorry... *what?*

* * *

Matthias

"This is your captain speaking. Please take your seats; we'll be landing in five minutes," Teddy calls from the cockpit of the private jet.

I'm sitting rigid in my seat, but Hutch and Canyon scramble to wrap up the card game they were playing on the table. Six of my brothers are with me. Everyone except Everest. He's refusing to shift to human, so we left him behind to keep an eye on Daisy and the mountain.

The triplets have behaved themselves this whole flight. Even Darius is helping Teddy in the cockpit, without their usual bickering. That's how I know everyone is taking this mission seriously.

Out the window, Vegas glows. To a tourist, it might look like one giant party, loud and bright enough to turn the night sky into a murky blue. To me, it looks sinister.

Between Wren's psychic abilities and Kylie and Hutch's tech abilities, we figured out that Maisy was most likely kidnapped by men working for Allen's boss, a man who goes by the dubious moniker, Lucky Lou. Kylie's still digging into him, but he's a small-time hustler with delusions of grandeur. He probably has something to do with this.

What we don't know is why Maisy's involved. It makes no sense.

They pinpointed Maisy's dad's apartment. He's been living below the poverty line on the edges of the city.

That's where we're headed. We can't get there fast enough. I'm grateful I have friends and family who banded together to figure out a good place to look for Maisy. Lana loaned us her jet, and Teddy got us here in record time, but the minutes it takes to land and get to the rental bus seem endless.

I carry my doctor's bag—I brought my emergency medical supplies, in case Maisy's hurt. I don't have a weapon, but I don't need one. My bear is more deadly than a loaded machine gun. I'm trying to be cool, but it's taking everything to keep me from roaring and shifting and smashing through the Strip on my way to hunt down Allen.

Mate, my bear reminds me.

We'll get her, I say. And then I'm going to release the bear.

We all cram into one giant party bus. When Teddy turns it on, neon lights start flashing and club music blasts out of the speakers, but Teddy hits a button, and the music stops. Not even the triplets are in the mood to party right now.

We speed away from the Strip as Kylie calls again. "I got a hit on Allen. Looks like he checked into a hotel near Fremont Street."

"That's old Vegas," Darius reports. "Off strip."

"Why would he get a hotel room?" Axel asks. "He lives here."

"Nothing confirmed, but hearsay says that the old casino next door is a known business holding of Lucky Lou," Kylie reports.

"Take us there," I say. "To the hotel."

"Should we split up?" Teddy calls from the driver's seat. "We can drop you off, and the triplets and I can go to Allen's apartment to check it out?"

"No. If Lucky's at the hotel, I might need backup." Maisy is our priority.

Teddy slides across three lanes of traffic to swerve onto the next exit.

"I have more information," Kylie says. "About Allen and Lucky Lou's plans."

"Can it wait?" I want to kill Maisy's father. It goes against everything I vowed as a doctor, and I don't care. If he hurt Maisy, he won't live long.

He didn't count on his daughter having friends. Or a werebear who's crazy about her.

The only reason I'd spare him is if Maisy asks me to. But I will make it clear to everyone that I will destroy worlds for her.

"You're gonna want to hear this. It's from texts between Lucky Lou and Allen. They took Maisy to settle a debt between them, and here's what they plan to do..."

Chapter Eight

Maisy

I huddle on the hotel bed, my head in my hands. Allen left shortly after dropping the bombshell, leaving me under the guard of the two thugs who picked me up in Bad Bear.

It's after one am, and I'm still groggy, but I can't sleep.

I felt well enough to take a shower and change into the *I heart Vegas* shirt my dad brought me. I figured I might as well do what I can to feel like myself.

In the morning, I'm going to marry a mobster unless I do something.

I need to think clearly to figure out a way out of this. Allen said he owes someone named Lucky Lou money, and in exchange for cancelling his debt, Lucky Lou wants to marry unlucky me.

"Don't trust atoms," I whisper a joke to myself. "They make up everything."

It doesn't help.

Like always, I imagine what it would be like to deliver

that joke to Matthias. What he would tell me to do in this fucked up situation?

Run.

But how? Can I somehow trick the guys outside the door into leaving? Or letting me get by? Maybe if I set a little fire near a fire alarm sensor, then it would trip the alarm for the building and the firemen would come. I scan the ceiling, spotting what looks like a sprinkler. That could work...except I have no matches.

Maybe I could bum a cigarette from one of the guards? I definitely smelled stale cigarettes on them.

I draw in a breath, trying to work up the nerve. I'm the girl who gets flustered when the hot town doctor walks into the cafe and orders coffee. Am I really capable of flirting with the low-lifes outside the door to convince them to give me a cigarette? I'm not Missy. I'm no actress. And even if I do convince them, I don't smoke! I'd probably gag and choke when he lit it for me, giving my scheme away.

But it's the only idea I've come up with so far, so I'll have to go with it.

I force myself to my feet and paste what I hope is a friendly smile on my face.

Just as I reach for the door handle, though, I hear the sound of a heavy thud, like a body got slammed against the wall.

I gasp, jumping back.

Another thud.

Is that good or bad?

The door bursts open. I swallow a scream.

Then I realize my fantasy has become reality, and Matthias is here. I blink. Maybe it's the sedative. Why would he be here? How did he find me?

"Maisy." He strides toward me, looking so big and dangerous, I can't believe he's real.

"Matthias? Is that you?" Shock turns to relief, and I burst into tears.

And then I'm in his arms.

"Shhh, beautiful." His deep voice rumbles through me. "I've got you."

"How did you get in? What happened to the guards?"

"I took care of them." He sits on the bed, still holding me tight, and I cling to him. He's so big and strong, I feel so safe even though Allen and Lucky Lou might be lurking nearby.

"Are you okay, beautiful?" He runs his hand down my side and then lifts my face up to him, so he can look into my eyes. He's not wearing his glasses, and his usual brown eyes flash with a blue light. He looks scary. Scary hot.

I rest my hands on his chest. The muscles under my palms are like granite, grounding me. "They drugged me with something. They just grabbed me and injected me with something, and I woke up here, and I'm so sorry...I missed our date!"

The corners of Matthias' mouth twitch like he thinks I'm cute. "Shhhh, I'm here now. And everything's going to be okay. Let's get you out of here."

He swings me up into his arms. I'm a big girl, but he lifts me like I'm light as a flower. Then he carries me out into the hall, where several of his brothers wait. The two assholes who kidnapped me lie in a crumpled heap on the floor. Darius is zip-tying their wrists together.

"Maisy!" Axel sounds relieved. It's so good to see him. Even though we don't hang regularly, he's always looked out for me.

"Hey," I say weakly.

I feel Matthias' muscles tense even further. "I got her," he growls. His voice is a deep bass that almost sounds inhuman.

Darius picks one of the thugs by the hair and drags him down the hallway where he shoves him into a supply closet. Hutch hauls the other one by the foot. I have a feeling they could easily lift them, but they want to give them the most ignominious treatment possible.

I find it immensely satisfying.

"Teddy's parked out back, and Canyon's in the lobby on standby, in case we need a distraction," Axel says.

"Let's go." I love how commanding Matthias' deep voice sounds.

Darius takes the lead, with Axel just behind him. Hutch and Bern close in behind me.

We move in quick formation down the hall.

"This way." Axel darts forward and holds the door open to a stairwell.

The bear brothers make it down the endless stairs in record time. I knew I was in a high-rise hotel, but I didn't realize I was on the twenty-fourth floor.

As soon as we reach ground level, Darius opens the door, and Matthias carries me out into the cool night, straight into a big white bus parked by the door.

Teddy nods from the driver's seat as we climb in.

Matthias sets me down on the bench seat at the back of the bus. The whole interior is glowing neon purple.

"Is this a party bus?"

"Yes," Matthias says. "It was the only thing that we could get quickly that would fit all of us."

"Oh." I let out a semi-hysterical giggle. I can't help it—after the strain and stress of being kidnapped, leaving with a band of bear brothers in a party bus strikes me as funny. And also awesome.

Teddy pulls away from the curb, even though only Matthias and I are in the bus. We've left his other brothers behind.

"Where are we going?"

"Nowhere for now. Teddy's going to just drive us around while I check you over. I want to make sure there are no ill effects from what they drugged you with."

"I'm fine." Even as I say it, I feel the heaviness in my body. The adrenaline rush of seeing him has ended, and I slump toward him. I can only sit there as he takes my pulse and blood pressure with the equipment he pulls out of his black medical bag.

"Pulse elevated, eyes a little dilated. How are you feeling? Any numbness, tingling?"

"No. I did feel dizzy a few times when I woke up. I'm just tired. Groggy."

"It is the middle of the night. That's okay, I have something that will help you feel better." He pulls out a plastic-wrapped syringe and preps it and a vial of some sort of medicine. The liquid looks clear, but when the light hits it a certain way, it has a red tint. "A dose of this will counteract the drug, okay?"

"Okay." I must look worried because he rests his hand on mine.

"Do you trust me?"

When he gazes into my eyes like this, I'd do anything for him. Follow him anywhere. "Yes."

He administers the injection, and I don't even feel it. Maybe I am a bit numb.

Almost immediately, energy rushes through me, like I

just went for a long hike, then drank a four-shot latte. "Whoa."

"It's potent, I know. It will heal you of any damage the drug did." He holds my hand. It's nice. "Tell me what happened."

I explain everything from the moment the strangers showed up at my door to waking up in the hotel room and my conversation with my dad. "He says this guy wants to marry me."

Matthias lets out an inhuman growl, and his eyes turn laser blue.

My eyes widen. I knew he was a bear shifter, but witnessing the signs firsthand sends goosebumps running down my arms.

"Not. Happening." His words have a snarl to them.

Damn. That's hot. So hot.

Is he growling over *me*? Would he make those sounds over any female from Bad Bear who got kidnapped?

Like...would he growl like that for Missy?

I want to think I'm special to him. When I was a teenager, I had this fantasy that one day Matthias would tell me that I was the woman he wanted and that he'd been waiting for years for me to grow up and be ready for him.

But that's silly. He's never shown any interest in me other than common courtesy.

"I'll rip that guy apart before I let him marry you."

Heat floods between my legs. I want to throw the back of my hand over my forehead in an old-fashioned swoon-pose and moan in a breathy Marilyn Monroe voice, "Take me, Matthias!"

Instead, I blush. Or at least it feels like I must be blushing based on how hot my cheeks and neck get. I clear my throat. "My dad says he owes a lot of money."

"Hey, guys?" Teddy calls from the driver's seat. "Wren called in a report from the hotel. Black Wolf helped her get eyes in the hotel, so she can monitor the mission."

"And?" Matthias keeps holding my hand, his eyes on me.

"Lucky Lou discovered his men were missing. He knows Maisy's gone."

I tense. "They'll be searching for me."

"They're not going to find you," Matthias says. His thumb strokes the top of my hand in a soothing motion. "And even if they did, they have seven werebears to contend with."

Werebears. He said it out loud.

Since the secret of Bad Bear mountain remains an unspoken one, I've never heard any of them acknowledge it. Not even the fact that Everest, the giant Polar-Grizzly who roams town, is clearly not a pet but a brother. I tried to ask Axel about it once, but he denied it, which hurt my feelings.

I turn to Matthias and rest my hand on his muscled chest. We're sitting so close together I'm practically on his lap, but it feels right. "Why would this guy want to marry me?"

"I don't know. But our friend Kylie's digging into him to figure it out. Did you know Allen used to have a trust fund?"

"What?" The words *Allen* and *trust fund* together don't make sense.

"His parents both came from money. He inherited his trust fund at age twenty-one and took off for Vegas where he spent it all as fast as he could."

That sounds more like the Allen I know. The one who hit his young daughter up for birthday money. "Allen's been broke as long as I've known him. But I guess I don't know him very well. I never thought he'd do something like this."

Matthias' eyes flash blue again, as bright as the neon party lights.

"Kylie's intercepted more texts," Teddy informs us. "Lucky Lou's calling in all his favors to find you. Whoever finds you is supposed to take you straight to the chapel."

I shudder. Less than an hour ago, I was scared and alone back in the hotel room thinking I was pretty much doomed. "I'm so glad you found me."

"I've got you now," Matthias says. "And I'm never letting you go."

My heart gives a double-pump. Um, wow. He probably doesn't mean that the way I want him to, but he's pretty much fulfilling all my teenage fantasies right now.

A look of steely determination comes over his face. "As for the marriage thing, I'm going to stop that right now," he says.

"You are? How?"

"You're marrying me."

Chapter Nine

Matthias
　　　　Dawn finds me in a tiny dressing room of the Las Vegas Little Chapel of Love, getting ready for my own wedding.

"Matthais and Maisy, sitting in a tree. Getting M-A-R-R-I-E-D," Canyon keeps singing. "Bern and Hutch join in, and then they all start singing "Chapel of Love" with full harmony and everything.

"Shut up," Darius growls.

"Let them sing." I straighten my collar. The white tux wasn't my idea—my brothers made it happen somehow—but I look pretty good. I turn and face my brothers, who have somehow sourced black tuxedo jackets and matching kilts. "They've behaved all night."

They even went out and picked up the marriage license. We had to call in a favor to get it, of course, but our contact Lucius can do anything, even convince a clerk to sign off on a wedding in the wee hours of the morning. It's good to have the Southwest's vampire king as your friend.

Our wedding will be official.

The moment I heard another man planned to marry Maisy, my bear flipped out. The Moon Cure barely kept me from spontaneously shifting and going on a savage rampage across Las Vegas, tearing apart every male who got near my mate.

The only way to calm my bear was for me to claim Maisy.

And since she's not ready for me to claim her bear style, my hope is that a legal claiming will soothe him enough, so I can function.

It has the added benefit of slowing or halting whatever plans Lucky Lou had for her. We don't even know why Lucky Lou wants to marry Maisy, but he can't very well marry her if she's already wed.

Not that I plan to let him anywhere near her.

When I glance in the mirror, my eyes glitter blue. I can't deny that my bear is ecstatic about what's about to happen.

Even if our marriage won't be real.

I need another dose of Moon Cure, but I don't want to pull out a needle in front of my brothers. None of them know I've been self-dosing for the past seven years to keep from going feral or claiming my mate.

"How's Maisy doing?" I ask.

"She's almost ready. The dress Lana found fits her." Darius pauses. "She has tons of energy."

Vampire blood will do that. I've been distilling medicines of my own from the potent blood of immortals. I've tested them on Daisy, with her consent, so I know they work on humans.

"Who's guarding her?"

"Axel."

A growl rumbles in my chest. Axel took Maisy to prom her senior year. I heard Daisy arranged it because she wasn't going to go, but that doesn't stop my bear from wanting to rip out his heart for being near her.

Darius holds up his hand. "Teddy's there too, but she wanted Axel. She feels comfortable with him."

I growl some more. I don't like that, At All. Axel says he's just a friend to Maisy, but my brother could be hiding a crush on my mate behind his quiet facade. Why else would he get so close to her?

"I have an update on Allen," Darius says. "While you were with Maisy, we went to his apartment but didn't find him. Kylie says Lucky Lou is blowing up Allen's phone, accusing him of taking Maisy. Allen's probably scared and on the run. He doesn't have the money to go far, so he's probably lying low. Should we go after him?"

"Later. I want all of you here as witnesses. This needs to look legitimate."

Darius doesn't question my logic. Lucky Lou has no idea who I am or that I have seven brothers. Even with a single witness, the wedding will look real enough to serve our purposes.

But I want my brothers here. There's no denying I want this wedding to be real. I want my mate to be bound to me by human laws, even if the marriage is only real on paper. Even though once Maisy's safe, the right thing to do would be to let her go.

For a few days, I'm going to pretend that I have everything I want.

"You folks ready to get this show on the road?" An older white guy in a gold sequin-covered suit jacket pokes his head into the dressing room. His bushy sideburns and thinning hair are dyed black to look like Elvis. He sees me and points his finger. "Oh yeah, there's the hound dog."

My bear bristles. *Dog?*

"Who are you?" Darius asks.

"I'm the officiant. Gonna float this love boat right down the canal. Put on your blue suede shoes, and I'll meet you at the altar." Faux-Elvis clicks his teeth, shoots his finger gun my way, and disappears.

"Huh," Darius gives me side-eye. "So, what were you saying about the wedding needing to look legit?"

"Shut up."

* * *

Maisy

My hands shake as I fix the white lace on the sleeves of my wedding gown. I don't know how Lana did it, but the dress she found fits perfectly. She must have called in a bunch of favors to wake up a Las Vegas designer at 3 a.m. and get them to deliver this.

I can't believe I'm about to get married in Vegas at an Elvis chapel. It's too crazy for me to even contemplate, so I don't.

The good thing is–I feel amazing. Whatever Matthias gave me has energy zooming through my body. I glance in the mirror to see my skin is glowing like I've spent a week at a wellness resort. I swear even my hair is shinier.

All this energy made my video conference call with Daisy go smoother. I swear she was seconds away from breaking down and weeping. At one point, Everest, who was crammed in our living room in his giant bear form, gave her a hug. Daisy's voice shook, and she looked every one of her ninety-two years.

I didn't know how to tell her I'm getting married. To Matthias. I kept it vague. I told her I was okay, and she should get some sleep. She looked like she hadn't slept last night.

I feel like I've lived several lifetimes between yesterday at 2 p.m. and now.

Someone raps on the dressing room door. "How you doing?" Axel asks.

"Fine." I try to reach the buttons up the back, but my arms are too short. "Actually, can you help me?"

The door opens, revealing Axel in a black tux. I gasp. "You look like James Bond."

"Except I do my own stunts." He swings his hair back, so it falls in a shining cape over his shoulders, and looks me up and down. "Maisy, you look beautiful."

"Thanks." I blush. Even though we're friends, I'm aware of how handsome Axel is. Everyone in my senior class had a huge crush on him. Even Missy, though she always acted like she didn't like him. "Can you button me?" I present my back to Axel, and he deftly does me up. I can't believe how well this dress suits me. The neckline is wide and very flattering, almost off the shoulder.

I smooth down the satin skirt and turn to face him. "How do I look?"

"Perfect."

"The triplets got me this." I show him the dinky plastic tiara with a little white netting for a veil. The "Bride to Be" sign pasted on the front is peeling off, and underneath it says "Happy New Year."

"I think we can do better than that. Here." He pulls a black velvet case out of his pocket and opens it to reveal a dazzling diamond necklace inside.

"Oh my God," I gasp. The necklace looks like something a celebrity would wear on the red carpet. Or a princess attending a ball. I'm not a princess...I'm not even Cinderella. I'm one of the mice scurrying around, holding a clipboard, making sure the wheels don't fall off the pumpkin. "Axel, I can't accept this."

"You can." Axel is quiet, but he's stubborn, and when he wants something, he gets his way. "It's a gift from Matthias. I guess he robbed a bank or something." He winks. "Turn around." He sets the necklace around my neck and does the clasp. "Perfect. It matches the ring," he adds, and I blush harder.

I can't believe Matthias got me diamonds. A real diamond ring and necklace with the papers to prove it–not a cubic zirconia or something. How *did* he get the money for them?

I can't believe I'm really marrying him. I mean, it's to protect me from some mob guy's crazy plan, but what even is my life right now?

A few rooms away, a microphone crackles and a man's voice booms out, "Ladies and Gentlemen, I want to welcome you folks to the little Las Vegas Chapel of Love. Let's get this party started."

"Who's that?" I ask.

"Elvis." Axel grins. He puts his hand on my back, guiding me forward, and we both glide out of the dressing room towards the chapel.

The triplets greet us at the door. I remember when they were gangly young guys with hands and feet that seemed too big for their scrawny limbs. These past few years, they've filled out. They're taller than all their brothers besides Everest, and so big and broad-shouldered, I can't see past them to the chapel behind. They're all so handsome, too.

"Who's going to walk you down the aisle?" Hutch asks.

"I'll do it," Canyon volunteers. Bern puts a hand on his chest and shoves him back.

"Maisy?" Bern looks to me. "You decide."

"Axel," I say. "You were my prom date, so you know the drill."

He gives me a smile and offers his arm. I take it.

"We'll be bridesmaids," Bern announces. The next thing I know, they're all holding matching bouquets of fake purple flowers. Where did they even get all this stuff?

Beyond the triplets, in the chapel, the wedding march starts playing. The triplets fight for a moment over who's going down first but then fall into line and disappear down the aisle.

Then it's Axel's and my turn. At the altar, Matthias waits for me, with Darius and Teddy by his side as best men. The twins are identically gorgeous in black tuxes, but Matthias outshines them all.

And me? I'm wearing a designer dress and tens of thousands of dollars worth of diamonds about to marry my longtime crush. Not even in my wildest dreams could I have thought of this moment.

Axel must feel how tense I am because he leans close.

"It's no big deal," he murmurs. "It's just pretend, right?"

"Right." I let out a shaky laugh. This will protect me. That's the only reason we're doing it.

But as he starts walking me down the aisle, it doesn't feel pretend.

It feels real.

* * *

Matthias

Some moments feel like years. Doing my first surgical

incision, holding a dying patient's hand, breaking the news to my mom about her illness–those moments stretched on and on into decades.

Waiting for my dream girl at the altar while Faux-Elvis performs an exaggerated version of "Blue Suede Shoes" took a lifetime. All the while, I'm wondering if she changed her mind. If she'll want to marry Axel instead.

It's not real, I scold myself. The ring is real. The paperwork is real, but they are the only things about this that is. I didn't even ask her to marry me–I told her.

She shouldn't trust me. If I had my way, I'd take her forever.

If she called this off, I'd have to walk away, and I don't know if I could do that. It's a good thing almost all my brothers are here because it would take all of them to stop my bear's rampage.

Then Maisy walks in, and all my worries disappear. The white dress and diamonds shine a spotlight on her beautiful face. Her blue eyes sparkle more than any diamond ever could.

I feel like I'm in a movie right now, one where everything is scripted exactly as my bear would like.

Except for one detail–her hand resting on Axel's arm. I watch him closely to see if there's any regret as he hands her over, but his face is perfectly composed. With Maisy in front of me, I can't focus on anything but her.

"Hey you," she whispers to me.

"You," I say because I've lost my ability to speak.

She scrunches her nose and gives me an adorable little grin. "What did Cinderella say about her missing wedding photos?"

I smile. "What?"

"Someday my prints will come."

I laugh softly. My chest squeezed. She was so cute, so sweet, so fucking innocent. I shouldn't be doing this.

Faux-Elvis breaks the spell. "Is this the bride? Little darlin', you're gorgeous. Ah-ah-ah I'm all shook up." He starts gyrating and thrusting his hips.

Teddy leans close to us. "Do you want us to kill him and bury him in a shallow grave?" he asks through gritted teeth.

I can't look away from Maisy. "It's fine."

The triplets apparently love it based on their wide grins.

"You ready?" I ask Maisy.

She smiles. "Let's do this."

Faux-Elvis starts rambling about love and marriage. Most of the speech is just the lyrics to "Love me Tender." I can bear it because it allows me to stand close to Maisy. I can smell Axel's scent on her. I stroke her soft waves back from her bare shoulders to replace his scent with mine.

No one else, I vow to myself. No one else is going to touch her from now on. Only me.

Oh fuck. My bear starts punching to the surface.

All that bare skin—there isn't enough Moon Cure in the world to keep me from stroking it.

I know there will be no wedding night. I won't be consummating the marriage. I don't have the right to strip her naked and lick her all over, and I'm not sure how I'm going to survive. My fangs are sharp and aching, ready to mark her.

I need her so badly. It hurts to breathe when she's not in the room with me, and now that I've touched her, I don't know what I'm going to do when I have to let her go. If I think about that, I'm going to throw her over my shoulder, carry her to the dressing room, and mark her. I'll rip her lovely dress to ribbons.

I'm going to need more doses of Moon Cure to get through the next twenty-four hours.

Right now, I just need to get through the next fifteen minutes without killing Elvis.

"What did the bride decide about the bouquet toss?" I whisper to Maisy.

Her eyes crinkle as she searches my face for the answer.

"It's still up in the air."

Her little smile is everything. The triplets, who can hear a whisper with their shifter hearing, all snort.

Finally, it's time for the vows.

"Now say, "darling, put your hand in mine." Faux-Elvis instructs, and I repeat the words, taking Maisy's hand. It's so small and soft in mine.

"And say, "All right, little mama, you lift me higher, you're the sun in my sky, the apple in my eye, and I don't want one more day to go on without you by my side."

Gazing deep into Maisy's eyes, I repeat the ridiculous vows and feel like I'm quoting Shakespeare. I feel them with all of my being. They're the words I've wanted to say for so long. "I'll give you the whole world. I've already given you my heart. And today I vow to be with you 'til death do us part."

"Matthias."

Just hearing my name on Maisy's lips makes my heart feel like it's going to punch through my chest.

"Love me tender and love me true. As long as you hold onto me, we can make it to the end."

If only I could hold onto her.

Elvis swivels his hips. "Uh huh. That's real good. Now slip that ring on and tell her she ain't nothin' but your wife now."

Axel hands me the ring. I cup it in my palm to replace his scent with mine then slide it onto my bride's finger.

My bride.

My wife.

Maisy.

Mine.

Maisy takes the white gold band that will be my wedding ring. Her hands are shaking, so I help her slip it onto my finger.

Elvis smacks his lips. "By the power vested in me by the great state of Nevada and the spirit of rock and roll, you may kiss your bride. Thank you, thank you very much."

Hell, yes, I'm going to kiss my bride. I'm going to kiss her until her toes curl.

Just to make it seem real, of course.

Not because I need to taste that mouth more than I need to breathe.

I cup her perfect face in my hands. She sucks in a breath. I can hear both our heart rates speeding faster. Then, they beat in sync.

I lower my head, ready to claim her mouth rough and dirty like the heathen I am, only barely stopping myself just before I touch her lips.

"May I kiss you, Maisy?" I murmur.

She stops breathing.

I stop breathing.

I've scared her. Fuck. She's way too intimidated to even know how to—

Maisy smashes her lips against mine.

I freeze for a moment, savoring the sensation. Savoring her consent. No, not just her consent—her desire.

Fate, how will I ever hold back?

It doesn't matter. I'm not going to. I switch my hands

from the gentle hold on her face to cup her nape and go in for the bear-kill. The searing kiss that will make her soak her panties and beg for more.

I immobilize her head, so I have all the control. My lips stroke across hers on an angle, once. Twice. Then I plunge my tongue between her lips to fuck her mouth with it.

She moans against my mouth. I drink it in.

That's right, beautiful. I'm going to teach you what a real mouth-fucking is like.

I suck her lips, scrape my teeth across them, plunge my tongue in and out of her mouth. I wrap my arm around the back and yank her body flush against mine, so I can devour her.

Too late, I remember she's probably never even been kissed.

She's Maisy. My delicate, breakable mate. My sweet, gorgeous wife.

I yank back, releasing her. My eyes must be glowing. My bear is right at the surface.

I study her face, expecting her to be afraid. Flustered. Undone.

Her eyes remain closed, lips parted. Head tilted back for more.

Fuck. Me.

I give her more. Another round of domination by kissing. Total mastery. Full ownership. I show Maisy how much she belongs to me with each lash of my tongue into her mouth.

This time when we come apart, she lets out a soft mewl of protest. Like she didn't want it to be over.

I'm so fucked.

I need more Moon Cure. Now.

My brothers cheer and applaud.

"All right, all right, let's get a picture of this hunka hunka burnin' love. Smile now!" Faux-Elvis instructs, and his assistant starts clicking so fast the flashes blind us.

Faux-Elvis starts singing "You give me fever," complete with leg shaking. The triplets join in with an off-beat cancan that has them kicking up their feet to make their kilts fly up.

I grab Maisy's hand, and we run to escape the chaos.

My brothers escort us out of the chapel, singing and laughing and talking nonstop.

"Wife," I say because I want the pleasure of calling her that. *Mate*, my bear rumbles, satisfied that I just had her in my arms.

"Husband." She grins up at me, and I feel like I could fly.

Chapter Ten

M^{*aisy*}

Matthias picks me up and bundles me onto the party bus.

"Make good choices," Hutch calls.

"Use protection!" Canyon says. He and Bern fight past Darius to open the door and throw in a handful of colorful condom packets.

I laugh because they make it funny rather than awkward. Now I know why people love Vegas. Anything goes.

Axel pushes them out of the way and slams the bus door, and Teddy pulls away from the curb.

My new husband sprawls next to me on the back seat. He doesn't mean to manspread, but he's so big, he takes up most of the seat and has to stretch his long legs into the aisle.

My wedding ring is a new, satisfying weight on my finger. The diamonds blaze, proof that the past half hour wasn't a dream.

If the ring didn't prove it, the puffy, well-kissed feeling

in my lips would. My new husband kissed the heck out of me. I can't stop smiling or touching my lips.

Matthias frowns, taking my hand to study my mouth. "Did I hurt you?"

"No," I laugh. Why would he think that? He would never hurt me. "It was just..."

"What?"

"It was my first kiss," I admit.

He looks stunned. Is he just now realizing how much of a late bloomer I am? Twenty-two and never been kissed.

"Maisy." He groans, and his head drops to his chest, and suddenly I'm worried.

"Is that okay? Was it a bad kiss?" I know he can have any woman he wants. He's probably been kissed a thousand times by partners way more skilled than I am.

"No. No, you were perfect. Come here." He pulls me onto his lap, and I don't fight it. I'm done fighting my feelings or being shy. The past twelve hours were the most harrowing hours of my life.

Why shouldn't I make out with my new husband? I've wanted to touch this man for years. I shift to straddle his waist.

His eyes shine blue. "What are you doing?" His voice is rough and gravelly.

"Practicing kissing with my husband."

For a moment, I think he hates it, based on the tortured look on his face, but then he smashes his lips against mine, kissing me again. It's incredible. Divine. He grips the back of my head for his plunder, parting my lips with his tongue.

Under my lap, I sense the bulge of his cock growing harder.

He's turned on.

I roll my hips, grinding against him.

"Fuck, Maisy." Matthias' hands tighten on my hips. His growl sounds inhuman. His eyes glow blue.

Does that mean he's turned on? By *me*?

With that encouragement, I go in for another kiss, using my tongue this time, the way he did. I start tentatively, just slipping the tip between his lips, then I grow more bold. The bulge of his cock presses up, warm and hard, right against the notch between my legs.

I rock my hips forward, grinding down on it. My panties instantly soak. Oh God—what if I leave a wet spot on Matthias' tuxedo pants?

Matthias' nostrils flare. "Maisy." His fingers tighten around my hips with bruising strength. Strain laces his voice, like he's afraid to lose control.

I don't know how it works with bear shifters. Maybe they only have sex in bear form?

Oh God, is it even possible with a human?

"Maisy," he chokes. His hands shift from my hips to grip my ass, and he pulls me down harder over his cock.

"Can we?" I whisper.

That look of alarm crosses his face again. "Can we what?"

My face heats, but I distract myself from my embarrassment by grinding on his cock again. "I just don't know how it works." My breasts are in his face, and his gaze drifts down at them. "Can you have sex with a human?"

He's breathing hard, his chest rising and falling like he was running a race. He uses the hands at my waist to lift my hips an inch away from his cock.

I'm tempting him—I can tell.

"We're not having sex." He sounds choked. A little angry.

I'd be hurt, but I know he wants me. I may be inexperienced, but I feel certain of it.

I kiss him again, sliding my tongue between his lips.

"Ow!" I draw back at a sting on my lower lip.

"*Maisy.*" Matthias' alarm is so great, he lifts me from his lap and sets me down on the bench beside him. "I cut you...." He swipes at my lip with his thumb, and blood comes away. "My fangs. Fuck."

I realize his canines have extended to bear length. I gasp.

"We can't." He looks every inch the grim doctor delivering bad news. "See? This is why we can't. I'm not safe for you, beautiful."

My pussy clenches, as if in disappointment. I try to stave off the pain. It's not a rejection, I remind myself.

Still, that familiar feeling of unworthiness soaks into me. It's the feeling attached to all the multitude of small and large rejections I received from my drug-addicted parents. I know from therapy they weren't related to my worthiness, but about their inability to function as decent parents.

"Fuck, Maisy. I want to. You know that, right?"

I nod, but the feeling remains. Sometimes you know something's true in your head, but it doesn't change the old familiar feeling.

"Come here." Matthias gathers me up in his arms and arranges himself sideways on the party bench with his back leaning against the side wall and his legs extending along the back bench.

He cradles me on his lap, pulling my head to lean against his shoulder. He cups my head in his big hand. I feel the cool metal of his own wedding band on my cheek and smell the comforting scent of his delicious cologne. "I just don't want to hurt you, beautiful. You're special to me."

I'm special to him.

Could it be my teen fantasy is coming true? That he has always been interested in me and was waiting for me to grow up?

Whether it's true or pretend, I choose to believe it.

The feelings of rejection and unworthiness seep away, transformed into a sense of safety. Of being cared for.

Of love.

That seems silly since the marriage is fake, and we hardly know each other, but I choose to believe it, too.

The effects of whatever medicine Matthias gave me have worn off, and I'm suddenly exhausted after staying up all night.

I tuck my face into Matthias' neck and breathe in his manly scent.

"Sleep, Maisy," he murmurs. "I've got you."

Chapter Eleven

Maisy

For the second day in a row, I wake in a strange bed. But this time, I know I'm safe even before I open my eyes. I smell Matthias' scent all around me. The memory of being cradled in his arms last night–well, technically this morning, but I'm calling it last night since I've slept between then and now–still makes me tingle all over.

I still feel amazing. The sun shines bright, high in the sky. I'm in a light, clean room that's decorated in light brown and soft blue colors to match the blue water sparkling outside the big bay window.

I'm wearing the wedding ring and the diamonds, but I'm wrapped in a fluffy bathrobe. The wedding dress hangs by the closet.

I guess I fell asleep on Matthias' lap last night. He must have carried me here and tucked me in.

The opposite side of the bed is still made, but there's a big dent in it, like a giant bear-man lounged there. He lay on top of the blankets, like a gentleman.

Maybe today I'll have the courage to ask him to take my V-card. Or at least find out why he's so afraid he'll hurt me.

"Good morning." Matthias walks in with two blue mugs of steaming coffee.

"Is it still morning? It was morning when I fell asleep."

"It's eleven." He offers me a mug.

"For me?" I accept it with a sigh.

"It's not as good as what you make, but I figured I'd start the day doing my duty as your husband."

Oh. My. God. He's calling himself my husband. I mean, he *is* legally my husband, but it was just to save me from my dad's scheme. Except now I don't ever want this to end.

I am definitely jumping this man's bones. I'm adding it to my New Year's resolution list. "Thanks, husband." I grin at him.

"Anytime, wife."

I pat the bed next to me, and he takes a seat. His weight makes the bed sink around him and tips me towards him.

"Did you sleep okay?" He peers at me like he wants to make sure I'm not going keel over.

"Yes. Where are we?"

"Lake Las Vegas, just outside the city. I didn't want to go far. I need to monitor you in case you have an adverse reaction to the medicine I gave you."

"I feel great. Better than great, actually." I feel ridiculously glamorous, lying in a mansion bed with a fortune in diamonds on my finger and around my neck.

Talk about a glow-up.

With a flash of guilt, I remember my real life. "Did Daisy call?"

"Not yet. She's probably still sleeping. Everest is with her, and Wren and Paloma promised to entertain her today."

That makes me feel better. "I'll video conference her later, when she's awake. Are your brothers staying here too?"

"They're still in town, keeping an eye on things." He keeps it vague, and I don't pry.

I should probably ask about Lucky Lou and my dad, but I don't want to. I just want to pretend everything's fine for a few hours.

"We're safe here."

"It's like we're on our honeymoon," I tease, but my face heats.

"That's right." The corners of his lips quirk, and I'm struck momentarily speechless by his handsomeness. He's not wearing his glasses, and while he's unspeakably hot with the black frames, seeing his face up close and unhindered makes me swoon.

I realize he's still talking.

"Pardon?"

"I said, you probably don't get a lot of time off from the cafe."

"No," I say. "I pretty much run things these days. Daisy's still the owner, and we have some great staff but..."

"You're the one who keeps things moving. I've noticed that. You also help Daisy with all her civic projects. Like Winterfest."

He...noticed that? He's noticed *me*?

The dreamy teen inside me squeals, *I knew it! I mean something to him. He cares.*

I squash her down before I embarrass myself.

"Don't get me started on Winterfest," I say lightly to cover my fluster.

Matthias chuckles.

"But you're one to talk. You work all the time. When

you're not doing shifts at the hospital, you're volunteering at the clinic."

"Guilty." He raises his hands. "I prescribe a day off. A real vacation. Doctor's orders."

"Yes, sir," I throw him a cheeky salute.

His eyes flash blue. Just for a second, but the color shift is so uncanny, it stuns me. Calling him *sir* affects him. Just like it does all those dommy heroes in the books I love.

But he continues talking, like nothing happened. "All right, little wife. What do you want to do on your honeymoon?"

* * *

Matthias

My gorgeous wife is going to be the death of me. We've only been married a few hours, and the first thing she wants to do after eating is...swim in the pool.

With *me.*

This morning on the party bus I nearly lost control. Maisy was rocking that sweet pussy over my lap. The scent of her arousal had my bear turning wild.

I wanted to throw her down on the bus bench and feast between her legs. Make her scream my name as I sank my teeth into her shoulder and marked her forever as mine.

But that would be wrong. So wrong. Her first kiss was at the altar! She may be legally of age, but she's still so very innocent.

And I want to do all manner of filthy things with her. I learned some disturbing things about myself when trying to find ways to blow off steam during med school. I learned I like to inflict pain. I love the sound of a leather strap across flesh. I like to hear the pained cry of a submissive in bondage. I need to play rough. I've imagined doing those things to Maisy...which is wrong.

So wrong.

Maisy doesn't deserve that kind of treatment. She's not ready for me and my bear.

I can't trust myself with her.

I wrap a band around my arm to get the vein to stand out, then inject a dulling dose of Moon Cure, change into a swimsuit, and head outside.

Lana had a whole wardrobe delivered, so Maisy has something to wear. But when she emerges from the house in a tiny yellow polka-dot bikini that flatters her curves, I nearly lose control. She's taken off the diamond necklace but is still wearing her wedding ring.

As she should be. If she were really mine, I'd order her to wear nothing but barely-there lingerie and her wedding ring when we're at home. It would mean cranking up the thermostat and paying a fortune in heating costs, but it'd be worth it.

Her shoulders hunch as she picks at the bikini strings as if wishing there were more fabric. She's probably nervous because usually she doesn't show so much skin.

"Maisy," I growl.

Her blue eyes fly to mine like she's alarmed at my tone.

I'll try to dial back the lust. The desire. The need to throw her down and lick between her legs until she screams. I clear my throat. "You look delicious," I say.

Oops. So much for dialing back. *Nice* would've been a better word choice. But it's true that I want to eat her up. Consume her.

She whispers, "Thank you."

Then she takes in my outfit. I'm in a brand new pair of board shorts that I found in the pool house. My friends

Lucius and Selene keep extra swimwear on hand for guests.

I'm a shifter, so it's nothing to be naked. But Maisy has probably never seen me shirtless.

She's getting an eyeful now, and my bear smugly notes the spots of color on her cheeks. The scent of her arousal.

Oh, fuck–that scent. How will I ever maintain control?

"Is that blood on your arm?" She points to the inside of my elbow where a drop of blood remains from my injection of Moon Cure.

I scrub it off. "Probably a mosquito bite," I lie. I don't want to upset her. Her mother died of an overdose in front of her.

Then she clears her throat and looks away–at the lake, the sky, the pool, anywhere but me. "Um, yeah, you look nice too. More than nice."

I realize I'm staring at her cleavage, imagining gripping her fleshy hips and pulling her against me. What would it be like to pinch those taut nipples and tug a little? To make her whimper with the mixture of pain and pleasure?

No!

Nope. No. No way. Not happening. I can't think that way about Maisy.

Last night was *her first kiss*. Her. First. Kiss.

So she's not even *close* to ready for the torrent of aggression and lust I would unleash on her if I don't hold myself in check.

I gotta get a hold of myself. "So...let me show you around the house."

"I'd love that," Maisy murmurs.

The mansion design is a faux-Classical style with Corinthian columns and balanced proportions. It's a little less gaudy than the surrounding homes because of the little details like the imported marble floors and mosaic tile around the pool. Even the landscaping is tasteful, designed for privacy.

"This place is amazing," Maisy says.

We're both not looking at each other, but all I want to do is look at her.

"A friend of mine owns it." Lucius, the vampire king of Tucson, isn't friends with many people, but he made an exception for me since I've treated his mate.

Lucius's soulmate, Selene, is a creature that defies legend. Lucius reached out to me and asked me to perform some discreet medical tests to make sure she's healthy. The shifter community has a deficit when it comes to doctors up to speed on the latest medical modalities and an even smaller amount doing the type of research I am. I obliged and pronounced her the healthiest person on the planet. And that's saying something because Lucius is immortal.

Since then, Lucius has become a benefactor of sorts. His funding of my research allowed me to pay off all my student loans and sock away the savings that I used this morning to buy Maisy the ring and necklace.

Our partnership has borne a lot of fruit. Lucius gave me permission to run experiments on his blood, experiments that led to me developing the healing serum I developed for my mom's condition and used on Maisy last night. He's my main donor, so he's more than repaid the favor for private medical care. And now he's provided us with a safe house. I'll have to send him and Selene a thank you gift.

I extend my hand to Maisy. "Shall we, wife?" I don't get to call her mate, but my dick gets hard every time I call her that. Even if it's only temporary.

"Okay, husband," she giggles.

It's a game to her. A joke. That's good. I can't tell her the truth about what she means to me. About all the dirty, devious things I want to do to her.

* * *

Maisy

He's holding my hand, his large fingers wrapped around mine like a protective bear daddy. Except I want him to transition from daddy-bear to bear lover. I want him to kiss me the way he did last night. Like he wanted to consume me. Like I was his reason to live. Not that I mind the daddy-bear energy.

I find any man who's older and highly competent hot.

At least that's what I told myself when I started lusting after Matthias as a teenager. I was fifteen when I went through puberty–a late bloomer. Still am, I guess, considering I just had my first date and kiss at age twenty-two. Who knew it would also come the same week I got married?

The Universe works in mysterious ways, I guess.

"Wait," he says. "We're forgetting something." Still holding my hand, he leads me to a small building next to the infinity pool.

The tile work in the pool area is incredible. The colorful mosaic reminds me of an ancient Roman bathhouse, but it's blue and green and shimmery like a mermaid's tail.

Matthias goes to a cabinet beside the bar and opens it to reveal a hundred different types of sunscreen.

"Wow, this place is well-stocked."

"Lucius is old-fashioned. It's important to him to be a good host." He pulls out a bottle of sunscreen and squirts a bunch in his hand. "Lube up, beautiful."

I bite my tongue. *Don't make a dirty joke.* "Right. Sunscreen is important."

Matthias starts rubbing the lotion onto his muscled chest, and it's like porn. All I can do is stand and stare.

Don't think about that...think about something else. Something not sexy.

"Skin cancer," I blurt.

Matthias quirks a brow at me.

"It's bad," I say because apparently being around my new husband makes me lose brain cells. I draw in a breath and exhale. "That's why we wear sunscreen." I focus on applying sunscreen all over.

"You've missed some spots." He turns me to him and rubs tiny amounts of lotion onto my nose and forehead. His touch is so gentle, but by the time he's done I'm breathing hard. "And...I think, right here." His fingertip points a splotch of lotion between my breasts.

We both look at it.

Is he afraid to touch me there? Isn't he a doctor? *And* my husband? I mean...no reason to be shy.

I play dumb. "Where?"

His eyes meet mine, and he quirks a brow. It's a stern one—like he knows I'm misbehaving and is giving me a chance to reconsider.

Mmm. Bear-daddy wants to spank me. I recall how he seemed turned on when I called him *sir*.

Maybe he's kinky, just like the heroes of my romance novels. As a twenty-two-year-old virgin who's never been kissed, I've had a lot of time to read. And imagine...things.

Butterfly wings flap in my belly.

Oh my God, I would *die* if he were kinky. As if he isn't already five-alarm-fire hot to me.

He brings the tips of his fingers to the dollop of

sunscreen between my breasts and brushes it sideways, onto my boob.

I hold perfectly still, waiting, hoping he'll continue.

"Did you get all along your bikini line?" His voice sounds thick. Raspy. Almost pained.

My pussy clenches. My pulse flutters at my throat.

"Um...no." My voice sounds breathy.

But then he becomes the buttoned-down doctor. He takes the lotion bottle from me and squirts some onto his fingers then applies it all along my side boob. Or inner boob. Whatever that part is called. His fingers sweep under the triangle bikini top, but in sure, business-like strokes.

Still, it turns me on, and I drag my lower lip through my teeth and bite back a groan. I'm pretty sure I just soaked the gusset of the bikini.

Matthias' nostrils flare. A muscle in his jaw jumps. His eyes flash blue. Then, suddenly, like at the altar, and the party bus, he changes. He slides his entire hand inside my bikini top, squeezing my breast roughly as he backs me against the wall of the pool house.

I gasp, shocked.

He grips my nape, and his lips crash down on mine. I cling to his forearms, kissing him back.

He pulls and rolls my nipple between his fingers at the same time his tongue lashes into my mouth.

It's so delicious. So impassioned. Everything I ever dreamed about with Matthias.

I whimper, my knees buckling.

"Bad girl." His voice is a growl as he pinches my nipple a little harder. "You shouldn't tease the bear."

"Oh!" I cry out at the sensation. It only hurts a little, but it surprises me. His reaction surprises me.

He instantly breaks the kiss, and I stare up at him with wide eyes.

His eyes glow laser blue. He wipes his mouth with the back of his hand, looking semi-feral. "Turn around." It's an order, dark and commanding.

More flutters ignite in my tummy.

I slowly turn away from him.

"Hands on the wall."

Oh. My. *Gawd.* I let out an inner scream of excitement.

This is really happening. Sexy times with my bear-doctor. My bear-daddy. The man who's occupied every single fantasy for the last seven years of my life. The only man I've ever thought about when I touch myself.

His hand claps down on my ass, and I jump, giving a little scream. I was hoping for more spanking, but he tortures me by only rubbing lotion across my back in long relaxing strokes.

I push my ass out and wiggle my hips a little. Maybe he'll spank me again.

He squirts more sunscreen into his palm and slides his hands down the sides of my lower back, then dips both hands into my bikini bottom and circles my bare ass.

I cream my bikini. I want to put my fingers between my legs and touch myself because my pussy's throbbing, but he growls, "Now me" in that same deep commanding voice.

He hands me the sunscreen he's using, one that's specially formulated for black skin. It smells amazing.

"Ummm, I can't reach."

"That's right, shorty." He smirks down at me, then sits on a stool. Why is everything he does so effortlessly sexy? I'm dying here.

"I'm not short, I'm fun-sized," I quip.

117

His chuckle fills the room. "Does that make me family-sized?"

Whatever you do, do NOT think about having a family with him.

"No, you're perfect," I say before I think. "That is, uh, I mean, perfect for reaching things on the top shelf."

I'm a dork. There's no hope.

But Matthias seems to like it.

I attempt to survive gliding my hands up and down his beautiful back muscles to coat them with sunscreen. I rub the defined V at the base of his spine and he lets out a low rumble that feels like a mini-earthquake under my palms. I snatch my hands back, afraid I annoyed him somehow.

"Careful, love," Matthias warns. My bear likes you touching him."

I get a glimpse of the tent at the front of his shorts and realize that the man likes it, too.

I head straight to the pool, but Matthias grabs my hand. "We have to wait fifteen minutes before we get in the water for the sunscreen to work." He guides me to the lounge chair in the sunroom.

I spread my towel and lay down but am immediately uncomfortable. How can I look sexy with my boobs sliding into my armpits? I shift, so my arms prop up my boobs, but I must look like a wooden soldier. And now I realize Matthias has been watching me probably this whole time. I stretch my arms out and over my head and pretend to yawn. Super smooth. "I guess we should talk about my dad."

"We don't have to."

I sigh. "No, I want to know what's going on." What better time and place for this, than lounging in a bougie sunroom on a gorgeous sunny day?

"My brothers are trying to track him, but he's disappeared. He hasn't shown up to his apartment. We think he's on the run from Lucky Lou."

Lucky Lou. My father, Allen, tried to sell me in marriage to a man named Lucky Lou. How much more sordid can the story get?

I look around me. I'm currently living my inspiration board, so maybe there *is* something lucky about Lou.

"When we find him, do you want to talk to him?"

This feels like a loaded question. "Do I want to talk to the drunk who has caused me nothing but grief?

"I don't know. I just don't understand why he did this. I...used to want a relationship with him."

""You have a kind heart."

"I guess, I always thought one day he'd wake up and realize he had a daughter. That he'd want me."

"Nothing your dad does is about you or your worth. He's a long-time drug user. That sort of abuse causes damage to the frontal cortex. And if he's ever overdosed, he might have sustained a brain injury. "

"I know. That's how my mom died." I bite my lip. "Sorry, I'm ruining our honeymoon."

He scoots closer, so our thighs are touching, and takes my hand. He's touching me more and more, and I love it.

What's more, I need it.

"You could never do that. I'm honored you're sharing with me."

I brush at my eyes. I'm not crying, just...a little emotional. "I'm sure patients do that a lot. Dump on you," I say briskly.

"Not really. I think I intimidate people. That's why I wear glasses–they remind me to put on my bedside manner."

"I was wondering what happened to your glasses. They're not prescription?"

"No, they're props."

I let out a chuff of laughter and imagine him putting on his glasses before entering a patient's room. "Like Clark Kent. You're Superman."

Shaking his head, he pulls me up and leads me out to the pool, effectively avoiding the subject.

But I don't drop it. Once I get in the pool, I swim around a bit. The water must be heated, and the winter sun is warm in Las Vegas, so it feels nice.

Matthias does a few laps, and I get to watch his giant body move sleekly through the water, fast as an Olympic athlete. Eventually he resurfaces, shakes the water out of his face, and finds a spot near me to lounge.

"You are like Superman, you know," I tell him."You came to my rescue. As soon as I saw you in that hotel room, I knew I was safe."

"You *are* safe," he says. "I'll never let anyone touch you again."

"You slept beside me last night."

He looks away. "I wasn't going to let you out of my sight. I shouldn't have—"

"No, I'm glad." I swim close to him.

A muscle jerks in his cheek. He doesn't lean away from me, but his whole body is tense. "I'm too old for you."

I blink. Is he trying to shut me down? But no—I *know* he's attracted to me. He wouldn't have kissed me the way he did if he didn't feel the same way I do.

"I don't care how old you are. I wanted to go on a date with you." I take a risk and keep sharing. "I never thought in a million years I'd get to. But on this year's New Year's resolutions I wrote "go on a date," and I imagined going with you. I know you might not feel that way about me–"

"I do," he interrupts. For some reason, he looks unhappy about it, though. Instead of us both rejoicing that we're mutually interested, he's acting like it's a problem.

"Maisy, like I said last night, I want you."

"Oh. That's...good, right?"

"No."

I wait, but he doesn't go on.

"It's good," I insist.

That muscle in his jaw works again. "I'm too ol–"

"You're not too old for me."

"I play rough in bed. I'm a bear, Maisy. You're human. You're young and innocent. Fuck, you'd never been kissed before last night."

Hurt lances through my chest. Still, I cling to his admission like I did last night–he wants me.

I want him, too. I just have to convince him I'm not as young and innocent as he thinks I am.

"I know you're used to women who are more experienced, but–"

"It's not that," he cuts in. "Maisy, I'm dangerous."

I lift my chin. "Not to me."

"*Especially* to you."

I think about the past twelve hours. How he's taken charge. Protected me at all costs.

Back in Bad Bear, he's friendly but guarded. What he told me about wearing fake glasses makes me think he's playing a role. And not to manipulate anyone but to protect us. Even around his family, he's always holding something back. Always in control.

What would it be like to make him lose control?

These are bad girl thoughts, but... I want to be a bad

girl. I almost died for frick's sake. Isn't it time I ask for what I want?

Instead of asking, I reach out and brush some water droplets off of his shoulder. The muscle bulges under my palm. "You don't scare me."

"Careful," he rumbles. "I bite." He flashes a quick grin, showing white teeth. His canines look a bit longer than usual. Is that his bear?

"You won't hurt me."

"Don't be so sure."

I think about the spank he gave me. The way he pinched my nipple. Is that the kind of hurt he means?

"Maybe I want...that." I slide my hands down his sides to rest on his hips. I'm being bold.

"What do you want?"

I lick my lips.

He stares at them like he wants to kiss me again.

Why have we wasted so much time not kissing?

I rise to tiptoe. He's so much taller than me—broader, everything, I have to pull him down to meet me, but he leans down willingly.

"I want you to be my first," I whisper against his lips.

His breath gusts against my mouth, and then he hauls me up in his arms, and we kiss like we need the air in each other's lungs to survive.

He holds me up like I weigh nothing. I've never felt small or petite, but I do with him. He makes me feel sexy, and it makes me brave. I hang onto his shoulders and rub myself against his washboard abs. Grinding on him. My hips move naturally. I dig my nails into his back, moaning into his mouth.

I'm out of control, wild.

"Maisy...we can't."

"I want to, Matthias," I cup his face. "When those men grabbed me, I was afraid I might die, and the one thing I knew was that I didn't want to die without this. Without being with you. I'm not dying a virgin. And I *definitely* want my first time to be with you. Teach me."

"Fuck," Matthias curses, his eyes electric blue. He yanks my bikini top down, baring my breasts. "You asked for this."

Chapter Twelve

Maisy

Matthias pushes me backward to the steps of the pool, his hands squeezing and cupping my breasts. I've never had anyone touch me like this. Normally I'd be shy about being topless outside, but Matthias growls exactly what I need to hear.

"No one's ever going to see you like this." He squeezes one nipple between his knuckles, his lips at my ear. "No one's going to touch you. Only me. Only me. You were made for me."

I nearly orgasm from that alone.

"Matthias," I breathe.

"You want me to teach you, sweet girl?" He sits me on one of the steps and slides his hands up my thighs.

"Yes, Matthias."

"Yes, sir," he corrects.

Oh my God! I knew it! He's kinky!

"Yes, sir."

"Are you going to be good for me?"

I nod.

"I need to hear another *yes, sir*." He picks me up by the waist and turns me around, setting my feet on the second step.

"Yes, sir."

"Bend over and give me that ass, my good girl."

Oh God. He's going to spank me some more! I'm impossibly excited.

I bend over, offering my ass up to the dirty doctor.

"Hands on the pool deck." He tears my bikini bottoms off. I don't mean he pulls them down, I mean *tears them in half* to get them off.

Wow.

"Show me that ass, my sweet little wife." He cups my ass and then slaps it, making me gasp. It doesn't hurt, but the sound shocks me.

I'm a big girl. My breasts are a handful, and my ass and belly are huge. Matthias runs his hands over my body, stroking every inch of flesh like I'm this perfect goddess emerged from the sea, and he wants to worship by touching me.

For once, I'm not self-conscious. I'm consumed with something more, something beautiful and overwhelming in the best way. My neurons always short out when he's around, but right now that's an asset. I don't have to think because Matthias has me. He's holding me. He's got me.

He wraps his forearm around my waist and hauls me back into the water. I let my limbs go loose, let the water flow over me. He maneuvers me as he wants me. I'll let him do whatever he wants with me because he's my body's master.

"I'm going to make you feel so good, beautiful."

"Yes, yes."

He steers me to the nearby wall and positions me facing away from him. "Put your hands on the side of the pool."

It's easy to do what he says. I grip the side of the pool, staring out at the lake. We're in a deeper part of the pool, so I can't touch the bottom, but I feel safe, like I just have to follow his commands, and everything will work out perfectly.

He cradles my hips in his large hands, and presses me closer to the wall. That's when I realize he's got me right in front of a jet.

"Now spread your legs, Maisy-girl."

I do, gasping when the jet hits the sensitive place between my legs. "Oh, God." I push myself back, but he's right behind me. He's taller than I am, so he can stand in this deep water, but I can't, and that means...I can't get away.

The intensity builds. Stimulation in my most sensitive place feels like too much at first, then fills me with a chaotic, restless energy. There's a waterfall roaring, rushing, and it's focused right on my clit.

"Oh my God, Matthias...I can't—"

"You can, beautiful," he growls, pressing himself against me. His long, hard cock is just at the right height to probe my ass cheeks.

Shaking, I lean back against him. Talk about being trapped between a rock and a hard place. There's nothing harder than the wall of muscle behind me. Except maybe the giant dick rubbing against me.

I push myself back while spreading my legs wider, allowing the jet to stimulate me. It's so intense, it won't take long for me to orgasm.

Especially with Matthias crooning, "That's it, you're my good girl. Show me how you let go," right in my ear.

"It's so much," I pant.

"You can take it." He pins me with his hips and frees his hands. One plucks my nipples while the other comes to cup my throat. "I want to see you come apart. You can do that for me?"

I nod.

"Are you close?"

I make a sound that's more of a breathy moan than a *yes*, but he gets it.

His hand tightens around my throat. "Ask me for permission to come."

What? My arousal blooms even hotter, which I didn't realize was possible.

"Please, please," I'm begging before I can think about it. "I want to come."

"From now on, you don't orgasm without my say so."

Oh. My. God. "Okay," I breathe, but he tips my head back, so I can see his stern expression. And stern Master Matthias is my new favorite Matthias.

"No, sweet. When I'm making you come, you call me *Sir*."

* * *

Matthias

There's no one more gorgeous than my mate. She's sexier in sweatpants than any porn star.

But half-naked in my arms, begging me for an orgasm? I'm so satisfied I might as well be in heaven.

Maybe my heart stopped at the altar, and I am in paradise.

She comes apart in my arms, cheeks stained with color, eyes wild. My dick is so hard, if I angle her right, I could drive right into her. Straight into the promised land.

But no. I need to wait because she's not ready. *I want you to be my first.* Because my little beauty is a virgin.

Fates, I'm going to *consume* her.

Her cries echo over the lake. She's begging me now, pleading for the pleasure to end. I'm going to get a lot of use out of this pool, but I don't think she's ready for orgasm torture.

She's limp in my arms, letting me fully support her weight in the water. I tell her how good she is, how glorious, how I've never seen anything so lovely. "What a gift you are to me." I stroke her breasts, toying with her hard nipples. I want to bite them.

Later.

I lift her and carry her from the pool, letting the water stream off of us. The sunroom overlooking the pool has sturdy lounge furniture that can endure the outdoor weather, so I'm not worried about it getting wet.

I set her on the sunroom double lounger and spread her legs to examine her. Her sex is pink and puffy, not just from orgasm but the pressure. I'm tempted to tie her spread eagle and feast, but...she's new. I need to go slow. I need to be gentle.

So I dry her off and lay down next to her. The chaise is large, built for two, but it creaks under my weight. I ease her half on top of me and stroke her wet hair until she blinks up at me.

"How are you feeling?"

"That was..." she huffs like there are no words.

"Good."

"You want me to call you *sir?*"

I groan, and my dick jumps in my shorts. Her eyes grow wide. "I felt that," she murmurs.

My groin is aching like I've been beaten.

"Do you need to come...sir?"

I'm going to come in my shorts if she licks her lips again.

"Soon," I say. "I want to make sure you're all right."

"I'm good. I"m better than good."

I cup her cheek. Her skin is hot with arousal, almost feverish. "You want to play some more?"

"Yes, please, sir."

I'm not going to be able to hold back.

"Get on your knees," I tell her softly.

Her gaze goes hazy again. She nods and slides off. I sit up and situate myself, so my cock is out, and my legs are on either side of her.

I take a handful of her wet hair and guide her closer. The rug here is thick, so her knees will be fine, even if I make her kneel for a long time. Every room in this house is designed with this sort of sex play in mind. The dom in me appreciates it.

She's breathing hard, staring down my cock. So I keep hold of her hair and tell her what to do.

"Put your hands behind your back." The position puts her chest on display.

I remind myself that I'm playing with a human, not a shifter. Maisy will bruise. But more than that, she's emotionally fragile. She could break.

"You can take a break at any time. Even if I've just given you a command. I don't want to push you."

She licks her lips again, making my cock throb painfully. "Oh, it's fine. I want it."

Fates, she's perfect for me.

"I know, beautiful. But it's okay to tell me what you need."

"I've never done this before."

She's killing me, but I'll die happy. "I love that I'm your first." First, last, *only*. "You can't disappoint me. You're already perfect."

That seems to relax her. Her shoulders drift down. I pull her head down by her hair.

"Grip the base and kiss the head, Maisy."

She obeys.

"Now, use your tongue." I shudder in pleasure as she tastes me, rolling her tongue around my slit. I want to come, but more than that, I want to watch her little pink tongue lick up and down my huge pole.

"Take the whole head in your mouth, beautiful, and suck."

Her lips part, and the warm, wet heat of her mouth engulfs the head of my cock.

"Poke your tongue into the slit," I order because I love the stimulation of my urethra. My hips jack up off the couch. "Now open, open wide. Take me into the pocket of your cheek first."

She's a fast learner, and she's driving me fucking crazy. The veil between my rational mind and instincts is thinning. Even though I dosed with Moon Cure before we got in the pool, I need more.

My fingers tighten in her hair, and my nostrils flare. Her gaze is on my face, watching for approval, so she must see her effect on me because she bobs her head faster.

The nails of her free hand score my thigh.

"That's right, beautiful. Dig your nails in. You can't hurt me. I like a little pain." So does she because every time I tug her head she sucks harder. Her cheeks hollow.

"Now take me straight back. Go slowly and relax your throat." I ease in until I bump her throat. She coughs, and I let her up, but she dives back on like she can't get enough.

"That's my good girl. I'm going to turn you into my perfect little cocksucker. My sweet little wife. You'll look so prim and proper by my side. No one will ever guess how you're the perfect little slut for me."

I watch her reaction to my dirty talk. Her chest rises and falls faster. She likes being my little slut.

But I like calling her a good girl best.

"I'm going to come," I warn her. "And it's your first time, so you decide. Do you want it on your skin, or do you want to swallow it down?"

She pulls off and licks her puffy lips. Her perfect, pillowy cocksucking lips. "Whatever you want, sir."

Dayum. I pictured her like this but never believed it would happen so soon. This fast.

"Mmmm, then I want both. Relax, beautiful, let your head release." I take her head in both hands and hold it still, thrusting my hips at the right pace. She lets me use her mouth. My balls tingle. "I'm coming," I warn her and erupt in her mouth. I pull out so just the tip of me rests on her tongue, so she'll taste me. She moves her tongue, stroking my sensitive head. I pull back and spurt onto her lips, her cheeks, then her chest.

"Fuck me, Maisy." I lean in and kiss her softly, catching my own flavor. Then I rub my cum into her skin and make her lick the excess off my hand. She does such a good job, flicking her tongue and giving me these breathy little moans like she's loving it, that by the time she's done, I'm ready to cum again.

I lean back, enjoying the sight of her on her knees. Her hands rest on my thighs, and she gazes up at me.

"What do you say when I give you my cum?"

She looks confused, but then figures it out fast. "Thank you, sir." She gives me a sexy little smile.

My virgin bride isn't quite as innocent as I feared. Must be all those romance novels she always has with her.

"Thank you for your cum."

Chapter Thirteen

M*aisy*

After he comes, Master Matthias disappears, and Bear Daddy returns to cuddle me on the couch.

"Are you okay, beautiful? Was that too much?" He strokes my skin.

It takes me a second to find my voice. I'm still coming down from the high of our first time together. "It was a lot. But no...I liked it."

"You know, I respect you, even when I have you on your knees, right?"

A tiny puff of laughter escapes my lips. "Yes."

"This isn't the sort of honeymoon you imagined."

"No." I sound dazed, so I give him a little smile. "It's better."

He's worried about hurting me. I'm going to prove to him I can take everything he gives me. I just came hard, and so did he, but the way his cock prods my backside tells me he already wants more. He's touching me lightly, stroking my arms and back, but it's making my pussy ache. He hasn't dicked me down yet, and while I'm a little afraid of the monster in his shorts, I need it. I reach between us to stroke his cock, but he stops me.

"Later. I need to feed you." He picks me up to set me on my feet, then leans forward and bites my ass before he stands.

Matthias sends me to rinse off in the shower while he orders tapas delivered for us. I come out in a bathrobe and find a healthy spread of small plates that we can nibble on all afternoon. I figured we'd take a break from the sexy stuff, but he finds a way to make eating erotic by setting me on his lap and feeding me. He catches my wrists when I try to return the favor.

"Do that again, and I'll tie your hands behind you."

"Is that supposed to be a threat?" I ask playfully. I had no idea I could be this bold. I'm embracing the wanton sexy goddess within.

"Careful, brats get punished."

Yes, please.

I wriggle in his lap, massaging his hard cock. "Don't threaten me with a good time."

He shakes his head, but the corners of his lips quirk. "I'll punish you later. You need to eat. And we should probably talk about limits."

"Limits?"

"Yeah, beautiful. What you like, dislike. And let's have you choose a safe word."

I lean back in his lap to study his face. He's dead serious. "It seems so...formal."

"It's to protect you," he rumbles. I rest my hands on his bare chest. He's still shirtless, and I appreciate it.

"I like you. I want to do what you want."

He tucks a strand of hair behind my ear. "You're a submissive, Maisy. It's even more important that you set boundaries with someone like me."

"The big bad bear," I mock growl.

"Exactly."

"What if I'm not sure what I like? Because...I'm new. I haven't..." My throat closes. Crap, he already knows I'm inexperienced. I don't want to spell it out for him.

What if I'm bad at this? He's probably been with dozens of partners, all of them more experienced than me.

"Whatcha thinking?" he prompts me, and when I tuck my chin, he puts a finger underneath it and gently lifts my gaze to his. I can feel his big brown eyes dissecting me. I resist the urge to squirm.

"I'm not sure if I'm going to be good at this," I whisper.

He doesn't answer me right away, just rubs his hands up and down my arms. His sigh rocks me. "Maisy, I want you to listen and hear me when I say this. You being bad in bed...it's not possible. I've wanted you forever. I've dreamed about you in my arms. If we don't do anything but cuddle for the rest of the night, it will already eclipse my wildest fantasies."

A shiver of recognition runs through me.

They weren't teenage fantasies. I was right. I somehow intuited that there was something between us. We were made for each other.

I sit with what he says and not just because he ordered me to hear him. I'm absorbing it, and already, I can feel it changing my beliefs.

Because he's not lying. I believe him. Matthias doesn't babble. He doesn't throw away words. I don't know if he was always this certain and secure in his opinions, but he's a man of his word.

If I think poorly of myself, but Matthias doesn't, well, Matthias is the smartest man I know. Maybe it's time I believe him.

Chapter Fourteen

aisy

The sun's hanging low in the sky when I end my video conference with Daisy. She looked a little better, if still pale. I promise to call her every day until I get back to Bad Bear. She obviously wants me back sooner than later but doesn't question me about it. I told her what Matthias told me about monitoring me for more symptoms, and she accepted it.

I don't tell Daisy about the wedding because I don't want her to get too excited and think it's real. We're going to dissolve it soon, anyway. It's not real. I don't want the embarrassment of her thinking it's something that it's not.

I also got to check in with Paloma and Wren, who gave me updates on everything. The cafe has a handful of part-time employees plus Ryan and Jenny, our two fulltimers. They can hold the schedule together while Daisy and I are out.

When I finish the call on the balcony, I step back into the bedroom and see a piece of cream-colored paper taped to the cushion. It's a handwritten note on silky card stock, and the commanding tone in bold, slashing script makes it clear who wrote it.

My beautiful wife,

Go to the bedroom and change into the outfit on the bed. Then follow the instructions on the next note.

Be my good girl, and I'll give you a reward.

—Your husband and Sir

My pussy is throbbing by the time I'm finished reading.

All through lunch I was dying to come, but Matthias kept me simmering on edge while we talked over some ideas for a scene and decided on safe words (red for stop, green for go, but he'll also halt and check in if I tell him to stop).

I could mostly ignore it during my phone call home, and after that Matthias was busy, and I'm not supposed to come without his permission.

Being a good girl only amps up my arousal. I like following instructions. And I definitely like being rewarded.

There's a red dress on the bed next to a second hand-written note. I slip off the bathrobe and put it on, only to realize it's less of a dress and more of a sexy baby doll nightie. The silky fabric slides over my skin, making me feel like a lingerie model. There's no bra or panties, just the baby doll top.

For a moment, I feel a flare of fear. Who am I to wear something this seductive?

Then the sparkling rock on my ring finger reminds me. *I'm Matthias' wife.*

Still, I feel a little nervous as I pad down the stairs to follow the instructions on the second note.

My beloved bride,

Follow the rose petals to the secret dungeon. I'll be waiting.

Your husband

Secret dungeon? Stuff's getting real!

There's a trail of white petals at the foot of the stairs, leading me down a hall.

Every step makes the baby doll skirt swirl around my thighs, reminding me that I'm bare. My New Year's resolutions were all about pushing out of my comfort zone, and here I am. Practically naked, so wet I need to clench my thighs together for a moment.

At the end of the hall is a bookshelf. There's another note instructing me to move aside a book—a collection of love poems—and pull the golden lever behind it. I do, and the entire bookshelf swings open, revealing a hidden door.

Goosebumps cover my skin. I follow the trail of rose petals—pink ones now—down an endless flight of stairs.

A final note waits for me on a pedestal. It's propped on a vase containing a single red rose.

. . .

Sweet wife,

Take this rose between your teeth. At the foot of the stairs, if you dare, crawl to me.

Your Sir

I have to pause and concentrate on breathing to keep from hyperventilating. I'm in a vast room lit by a chandelier and candles flickering in standing candelabra. There are large pieces of polished wood furniture that would look more at home in a medieval dungeon than a modern home.

This is the playroom. The candlelight gives it an other-worldly feel, and I don't feel like myself either. I feel like the main character in a fantasy story who crawls through a portal to find a new life beyond.

Matthias is across the room. We're alone. It's just us. And that makes it easy to do as I'm told and drop to my hands and knees. I crawl across the room, following the trail of red rose petals. The carpet is thick and plushy, but it's still a challenge. Thoughts drift through my head–this is silly, I probably look stupid, why am I doing this? But then I imagine Matthias saying, *Good girls get rewards.*

I know why I'm doing this. Because he told me to. And obeying him makes my pussy so very wet. My inner thighs are sticky, and any embarrassment I feel is swallowed up by the pounding ache in my pussy.

Still, it's a relief when Matthias' bare feet come into

sight, and I can kneel up. I keep my head down, savoring the feeling of submission. My head goes quiet.

I'm his, he wants me, and all is right with the world.

He takes the rose out of my mouth and lets it drift over me, caressing me with the petals.

"Good girl," he murmurs, brushing the rose over my lips. I could come from that alone. He crouches down and draws my head back by my hair, so he can kiss me.

"You're mine now, Maisy." He speaks the words like they hold significance then lifts my hair and clasps a necklace around my neck. The diamonds sparkle to match my ring.

Oh my God! He's collaring me. I'm officially his submissive. I've read about this. So hot!

"Crawl to the bed."

He waits for me to take the lead. I put one hand in front of the other, feeling the air brush my bare pussy. The nightie has ridden up to my waist, and I'm giving him an eyeful. Instead of feeling embarrassed, I let my hips sway.

I'm rewarded with a groan. "You crawl so beautifully." He brushes the rose over my backside, and I have to stop and dig my fingers into the cream carpet fibers, so I don't orgasm on the spot.

Something snaps against my upper thighs. The rose stem. He whipped me with the rose stem.

"I didn't tell you to stop."

Oh wow. Yummy. I waggle my hips as I crawl, hoping for another spank, but it doesn't come.

Somehow, I make it to the bed. He helps me up, holding my hand like I'm a lady and not a submissive who just crawled for him. I'm both, I guess.

"You're glorious," he tells me. He is, too. He's shirtless

again, with all his chest muscles on display. He's got black leather pants slung low on his hips.

I'm suddenly viciously jealous of every woman he's ever played with.

He pushes me to my back on the bed and drags the hem of the teddy up to reveal my bare sex. "Mmm." He brushes his thumb lightly over my labia, and I shiver.

I want more. So much more.

He drags his middle finger along the slit, parting my nether lips. I'm wet–juicy wet–so the movement drags slick moisture from my entrance up to my clit. He gives it a quick circle and then a tap.

"Show me how you touch yourself, Maisy."

My gaze seeks his. "Um, I'm not sure. I don't do it much."

He arches his brow. He's in Master Matthias mode, and I love it. "How do you make yourself come?"

I think of all the times I've made myself come. Every time I was imagining a moment like this, with him. "I, um, ride a pillow."

"Roll over," he commands.

I comply, and he promptly smacks my ass.

"Oh!" I jump.

"What do you say when I give you an order?" He slaps the other cheek.

"Thank you, sir!" I exclaim, trying to get it right. "I mean, yes, sir."

"Good girl. Lift your hips." I do, and he pushes a pillow under them and between my legs.

He smacks my ass again several times, but lighter than before. "This is a good girl spanking," he tells me. "To stimulate your erogenous zones and help you let go."

I surrender, relieved I hadn't disappointed him. The

spanks are stingy and warm but not painful. He's right, they do stimulate my pussy and my anus.

"That's it, beautiful," he purrs, stopping the spanking to rub and massage my ass. "You're a good girl, aren't you?"

"Yes, sir."

His fingers delve between my legs. It seems impossible, but I'm even wetter now, and he drags my slick up to my clit and circles the swollen bud. "What do you think about when you make yourself come?" he asks.

I moan. I've lost the ability to speak. It feels too good.

But Matthias slaps my ass, sharply this time.

"Sorry, sir! I, um..." Am I really going to admit it? Screw it, why not? "I think about you."

* * *

Matthias

I freeze as my bear roars to the surface. The Moon Cure is burning off fast. I shouldn't need more so soon, but I didn't expect her to reveal all her secrets to me.

My fangs are so sharp, they're aching. I'm ready to savagely claim her right here, right now. To sink my teeth into her flesh and forever claim her as mine.

She thinks about me.

Biologically, it makes sense. My bear recognized her scent as my fated mate. She's not a shifter, but on some level, her body must've known its master. I'd always suspected the reason I made her so flustered and nervous as a teen was that some part of her knew we belonged together.

The moment I have my bear under control, I crawl over my lovely mate, trailing kisses along her shoulder as my fingers reach under her hips. I cup between her legs, and even though she's a virgin, her body welcomes my index finger inside her.

"You think about me, beautiful?" My voice is a dark rumble right beside her ear.

I want to fuck her so badly it hurts. But I can't. Not until she's ready. Not unless I'm absolutely sure I won't fuck up, lose control, and hurt her.

"Yes," she breathes. "I always have."

Oh, fuck. My lengthened canines graze her shoulder. Even though I want to breathe in her cinnamon and caramel scent, I pull my head away to avoid the temptation of accidentally on purpose marking her. I roll my hips against her ass, positioning the bulge of my cock between her legs as the heel of my hand grinds down on her clit. I stroke in and out of her with my index finger, widening her entrance, training her to take my cock.

"Am I doing this in your fantasies?" I nip her ear and tug.

Her thighs start to tremble beneath mine. She's almost ready to come.

"Um..."

"Do you remember the rule I gave you, beautiful?"

"Hmm?" She wriggles her hips. Her inner thighs squeeze around my wrist.

I make my voice stern. "You don't come without my say-so."

"Oh." She stops grinding, but her inner thighs still quake, like she's trying, but failing to relax.

I decide to keep edging her and change up the position before she comes.

Time for a little pain.

I lift off her and pull the pillow out from under her hips.

"Roll over, sweetness. I'm going to help you remember to behave."

Maisy rolls over. Her cheeks are flushed, her blonde hair falls across her face. Her eyes are glassy and dilated. My female is in the throes of lust.

I pick up her ankles and lift her hips in the air, exposing her ass. I don't spank her hard. Just a light titillation to set every nerve ending on fire.

She pants and wriggles, letting out little cries and mewls that nearly make me jizz in my pants. Despite my pleasure in mastering her, I don't have the urge to cause her real pain. I'm only interested in her pleasure.

All the times I dommed males and females there, I never once had sex with them. I never let them see me come. From the moment I realized Maisy was mine, I saved my orgasms for her.

It seems Maisy has done the same. All this time, I've been the only one for her. Perhaps she's not so much a late bloomer or as innocent as I thought. Perhaps she's just been waiting all this time for her one true master.

Me.

When her ass is a perfect hue of pink I stop and rub, sweeping my palm in a circle around her plump globes.

I part her legs. "Bend your knees, beautiful."

She obeys, and I push her knees up toward her shoulders, lifting and spreading her for me.

"I need to taste my wife."

I lower my head between her legs and lick into her. Her pelvic floor muscles squeeze, and her thighs jerk closed at the sensation. I hold her open and take my time, tracing inside her labia with my tongue.

She mewls, shivering.

I flick the nub of her clit, and her hips jerk. When I affix my lips over the little nubbin to suck, she shrieks, bringing her hands to my head.

"Matthias...Sir...oh my God."

"That's right, beautiful." I lift my mouth only to growl my approval of her pleasure-taking then return, sucking her labia.

When her pelvic floor contracts again, I say, "You want something inside you, don't you, sweet girl?"

"Uh huh...yes, Sir," she moans.

I lick my index finger and screw it inside her. Her channel is tight, and my digits are thick, but she takes it. I push all the way to my last knuckle. "Good girl. You're taking it so deep, Maisy. Ready for two?"

"Yes, sir." She has the wanton minx moan down pat.

My dick throbs painfully, pressing against the zipper of the leather pants I found in Lucius' playroom closet.

Fuck.

I don't know how much longer I can play with my sweet wife before I lose control of the bear.

I work two fingers inside her and curl them up to stroke her inner wall. I locate her G-spot—the place where the tissue tightens and wrinkles under my fingers, and I massage it.

She goes wild, moaning and thrashing her legs as her pelvis jerks.

"Do you need to come, Maisy-girl?"

"Yes! Yes, please! Yes, sir!" she cries out.

I pump my fingers, making sure I hit her G-spot with the tips of them every time. She squirts in a glorious female ejaculation, and sobs, "Please...please. I need it!"

"Come for me, beautiful." I keep pumping. "Hold your breath while I count to three," I say because holding the breath can speed the onset of an orgasm. "One...two...

three." I push my fingers inside her and hold them there, stroking her G-spot.

Maisy screams, her pussy squeezing around my fingers, her legs shaking. She's glorious. Magnificent.

Mine.

Mine!

Fuck, that's my bear, roaring to the surface. I suck in a sharp breath and puff it out.

Not yet, I tell him.

Not. Yet.

Even though she's clearly all in with receiving sex lessons from her new husband, she's still young and vulnerable. She's damaged from early childhood trauma before Daisy got custody.

If I claim her now, I'd be taking advantage of a young woman who hasn't received enough attention and is easy to manipulate.

I shouldn't. It's not right. Some day, maybe not tomorrow but maybe in ten years, she could grow up and realize she got bamboozled into mating a dominant male who is way more than she can handle.

Maisy collapses back on the bed, wrung out from her orgasm, and I ease my fingers out and lick them.

"I'll be right back, beautiful."

"Okay," she murmurs sleepily.

My bear snarls, furious that I'm leaving her.

Stay. Down.

I have to get to my medicine bag and shoot up with Moon Cure again.

Fuck. I thought I could handle touching my mate, but this is getting impossible to manage.

Chapter Fifteen

Matthias

I leave Maisy sleeping to inject more Moon Cure. It's the middle of the night, but I don't trust my bear, not with my sweet wife sleeping next to me.

While I'm up, I check my phone. Lucius called soon after sundown, which would be when he rises.

I return his call immediately, which is the courtesy the ancient vampire deserves. Once I've caught him up on everything, he offers his help, and I tell him I'll take him up on it when I know more about how we're going to deal with Allen and Lucky Lou.

"And how are you finding the lake mansion?" Lucius turns the conversation to a happier subject. His accent has softened, but he still sounds Old World. Because he is.

"It's fabulous. And thank you for letting me know about the playroom. We made good use of it."

"No need for thanks." He sounds satisfied. He loves being a good host. "I'm glad you're enjoying yourself. I'm sure your new wife enjoyed herself too."

"I made sure of it. She's sleeping now, or I'd have you meet her."

"Worn her out already?" Lucius runs the best dungeon on the West Coast–Club Toxic. Not that I've played there. I haven't touched a female since the day I realized Maisy was mine.

I peek back in the bedroom, where Maisy is still slumbering. "No comment."

He chuckles. "I'm sure you are training her the way you want."

Guilt flashes through me. I glance back at Maisy. Her eyelids flutter with the telltale signs of REM sleep. Her lips are swollen from my kisses, and under the blanket, I know her vulva is too.

I've probably pushed her too hard. She wanted it, but she's so inexperienced. I should've slowed down.

She loved it. She came hard. But...I can't shake the feeling that a normal boyfriend would've been gentler with a new partner, who's a virgin to boot.

My bear growls at the thought of anyone else touching her. He's prowling in the background, ready for my control to slip, so he can pounce on my wife and mark her. My fangs throb with the need to sink into Maisy's sweet skin.

Fates, I just took Moon Cure. Do I need a double dose?

Lucius is still talking, so I tune back in.

"--assume she's your mate?"

"She is, yes."

"How fortunate we are, that Fate provides a perfect match for us. And you found her so early in your lifetime."

I stiffen, thinking he's talking about how I found Maisy was my mate seven years ago.

Then I remember, he doesn't know. No one does. And it's a secret I intend to keep, even from my wife.

Lucius sighs, like he's remembering the millennium he waited for his mate. I don't actually know how old he is, but I'm grateful I found Maisy in my twenties. Even if I had to invent Moon Cure to stay sane. Seven years is nothing compared to a thousand, but either way, she's worth the wait.

"There's something I need to talk to you about. I'm going to need more hemoglobin from you. A few liters, at least." I hate asking for so much, but I need it to distill Moon Cure.

"For your patients?" Lucius knows I've been treating both human and shifter patients with compounds made from his blood. He doesn't know it's Daisy and my own mother,

"For me." I fight my desperate feelings and explain to him about Moon Cure.

Lucius is silent for some time after, digesting this information. I fight the urge to say anything, to assume he's angry or off put by me using his blood for my own medicine.

"This mating cure...does it work?"

"It's worked so far." I dig my nails into my palm and notice that they've grown to claws. I have to focus before they retract.

My bear is close to the surface.

"That is extraordinary." Lucius doesn't sound awed, but his tone is always pretty dry. "A medical breakthrough."

"Yes." I'm relieved he thinks so. "All made possible by your blood."

"You shall have what you need," he pronounces, like it's a royal decree. "It will take me a few moons to gather that amount of blood."

I wince. I'm down to my last few doses of Moon Cure,

and it'll take a few days for me to distill more. "I need it as soon as possible."

"I will do my best. It is not my place, but may I ask...is it wise for a shifter to put off mating?"

I close my eyes and rub my forehead. When I open them, they're glowing blue in the bathroom mirror.

"You will forgive me for asking, Matthias. Selene and I consider you a friend, and as such, you are precious to me. To us. That is why I ask if this Moon Cure is safe."

"No." My voice is bear-rough. "But I need it."

"Why?"

"My new mate is human. Fragile."

"Ah yes, I understand. You are afraid of hurting her. Of going too far."

It seems so simple when he sums it up that way. It's so much more. A lifetime without Maisy. Of knowing I hurt her...and that I deserve to be alone.

I clench my fist, which I just noticed is shaking. "Do you think—"

But before I can ask him for advice on handling a fragile human sub, Maisy lets out a soft, distressed sound. I end the call quickly.

By the time I race to her side, she's thrashing in the sheets.

"Sshh, beautiful, it's okay." I draw back the covers to free her. She wakes with a start, her eyes wide. Her heart is racing.

When she sees me, she startles.

"Maisy, it's me. Matthias."

"Matthias," she whispers, sounding broken.

I sit close and reach for her. "Can I hold you?"

At her nod, I pull her into my arms. "Bad dream?"

"I was back in the casino hotel. The door opened, but it was my dad. You didn't come—it was too late." She lets out a shuddering sigh.

I just hold her, letting her come back to the present. "I'm here now, beautiful. No one's going to hurt you ever again."

I feel her head bob under my chin.

"You ready to go back to sleep?"

"I think so. What time does a duck wake up?"

"When?"

"At the quack of dawn."

I laugh softly. "That's my girl. C'mere." I lay her down and wait until she's comfortably situated on her side, facing me. The bedside table holds rope, I take her wrist and do a simple single column tie. I make it loose enough she can wear it all night, and use my phone flashlight to check her fingertips for capillary refill.

Then, I make a loop and slip it around my own hand. "There. Now you can't get away. And if anyone tries to take you from me, I'll know." I'll wake up long before an intruder finds the bedroom, but I can tell how comforting the rope is by the way she relaxes.

"Thank you, Daddy," she whispers, and drifts off to sleep.

My cock goes rock hard.

No. No, she didn't.

I've never been into daddy dom play. Before I knew Maisy was my mate, I was more of a sadist. But her calling me daddy gets me hot.

Gah. Either way, sadist or daddy dom, I'm a deviant. I shouldn't foist my twisted kinks on my sweet, innocent mate. I can't take her calling me Daddy as a green light to fully claim her and do all the filthy things I can imagine with her.

No, I still need to hold back. Keep taking the Moon Cure.

Stay in control.

Chapter Sixteen

atthias

The next morning, I wake up with Maisy curled in my arms. My mouth is pressed to the curve of her neck.

Only the diamond necklace saved her from me marking her. The necklace that I put on her like a collar, hoping it would satisfy my bear as a substitute claiming.

I rip myself away from her side before I do the unthinkable.

I need more Moon Cure, *now*.

My harsh movement jostled Maisy. She rouses, looking dazed. She's in nothing but the diamond necklace and everything in me aches to return to the bed, to gather her soft body into my arms.

"Matthias?" She blinks but doesn't sound frightened, the way she did when she woke in the middle of the night.

"I'm here, beautiful. Go back to sleep." I curl my hands into fists, and my arms shake with the need to go to her. Instead, I head to the bathroom to get another dose of Moon Cure.

A double dose.

This time the serum burns in my veins. It feels like ice spreading through my body. Acute pain shoots through my aorta. I clutch at my heart, willing it to keep beating. *Potential side effect: arrhythmia.* I'll need to make notes.

Maisy is still awake when I re-enter the bedroom.

"How are you feeling, love?" I climb onto the bed beside her and wrap an arm around her waist.

She stretches. "I feel great, Doctor. Want to examine me?"

Thank fate I just took a dose of Moon Cure, or I'd push her down and maul her with my cock and teeth.

"Oh, I'll be subjecting my little wife to plenty of examinations," I tease, lightly running my palm up her belly to cup her breast. Her butterscotch and cinnamon scent is an addiction I don't want cured.

She rolls to face me. "What made you want to become a doctor?"

I brush her hair back from her face. "My parents died in a car crash when I was young. Winnie was my adopted mom–you probably knew that."

She nods, her big blue eyes trained on my face.

"I felt so powerless. I'm sure you experienced something similar when your mom died."

Compassion fills her gaze, and she nods again. "I watched it happen," she croaks. "I called 911, but it was too late."

"Fuck." I pull her body against mine. "That's so horrible. You know it wasn't your fault, right?"

She nods. "Daisy got me in therapy right away, which helped." She rests her hand on my chest. "So what happened with you?"

I clear my throat. "Shifters have spontaneous regeneration. It's hard to kill us. But my parents' death put the fear of losing someone else I loved into me. Winnie...or my brothers.

So I guess I thought studying and understanding medicine would allow me to control any situation like that, if it ever came up."

Maisy's lips twitch. "You do have a controlling side, don't you?"

I flick my brows. "Believe it."

"I memorized dad jokes; you became a doctor."

"Your coping method was far less costly and time-consuming," I tell her wryly.

"But you love your job."

I smile. "I do." I shrug. "I like helping people." I flick my brows. "And being in charge."

Maisy's smile is wanton. She responds to my dominance like she was made for it.

But I hope to Fate I haven't implanted too much of my kink and desires on her. She's receptive, but how could she really know what she wants if I'm her first? I don't fully trust myself and my desires, and I've had way more experience that she has.

I kiss her forehead. "Now you stay here, and I bring you breakfast in bed. I need to feed my wife, so she has the energy to put up with my demands."

Maisy's nipples get hard, and the scent of her arousal makes me growl, but I force myself to leave her in bed.

I'm making coffee in the kitchen when I hear a motorcycle pull up outside the house. I knew one of my brothers was going to check in sometime today, but I didn't realize it'd be Axel. His scent makes me clench my jaw. I still haven't forgiven him for befriending Maisy.

I meet him in the lounge area near the door. He raises

his face and sniffs the air. I don't need to explain what we've been doing. He can smell it. The sweet scent of Maisy's arousal perfumes the place.

I wait for him to comment on it, but he just asks, "How is everything?"

"Good. Maisy's resting. How's Vegas?"

"We're lying low. The triplets are bummed they're not allowed in the casino yet. They wanted to use fake IDs, so they could do slot machines, but Darius stopped them."

"That's probably for the best."

"Canyon made him promise to bring them back for their birthday. Hutch and Bern are already practicing counting cards."

I shake my head at the thought of the triplets hitting Vegas for their twenty-first birthday.

"We're still surveilling Lucky Lou and his men. Are you ready to make a move on them?"

"Not yet. But soon. Let's find Allen first, and then we'll take care of them." Lucky Lou and his henchmen aren't long for this earth. They touched Maisy. They have to pay.

"Got it." He hesitates like I'm not going to like what he has to say next. "I'd like to talk to her before I go."

"She's taking a nap."

"I'll wait." He leans against a couch arm, folding his arms across his chest.

"You misunderstand." I face him down. I'm taller than him, and I'm not above using all my height to intimidate him. My bear wants to speed across the room and rip off his head, and I want to throw him out on his ass just for breathing Maisy's scent, so asserting dominance is a nice compromise. Only the Moon Cure holds me in check. "I don't want you bothering my wife."

"Your wife," he repeats, as if wondering if I mean it. His

forehead creases as he stares into my eyes, hard. I'm more dominant, so after a moment, he drops his gaze.

But he doesn't back down. "I'd like to talk to Maisy and make sure she's okay. That this—" he twirls a finger as if indicating the smell of sex hanging in the air— "is okay. Because she didn't sign on for any of this." Now his eyes flash bright green. His bear is out.

"I know that."

"But you're fucking her like it is real. Does she know what this is? Does she know that she's your mate?"

My guilt tears at me with vicious fangs. "None of your business."

"It *is* my business. I want to know if you're going to commit to this, commit to her, or forget all this happened once you're back home."

"What does it matter to you?" My eyes are bright blue. He can see my bear is out of control. I'm feral.

But he stands his ground. "Maisy's my friend. If you leave her, I'll be the one who has to pick up the pieces."

"Is that what you're waiting for?" I advance on him. "For me to leave, so you can swoop in and be her hero?"

I don't let him answer. I cross the room and shove him back. "What's your intentions toward my wife?" I snarl. "You took her to prom. All the years of picking her up and taking her for drives. Little escapes just when she needed it the most. How long have you been watching her? Wanting her? Are you carrying a torch for her?"

"No." He bares his teeth at me. If I hadn't taken a double dose of Moon Cure, I'd treat it as a threat and rip his head off.

I circle him, and he turns to face me, his eyes bright with his bear. "Then why did you get close to her? Did you want her?"

"No!" But he presses his lips together. He's holding something back, and I'm going to get it out of him.

"I don't believe you. You told me she was perfect. That the person who ended up with her would be lucky."

"That's true."

"So why don't you want her?"

"Because her best friend is my mate," he growls.

I stare at him, chest heaving. We're both breathing hard. "Who?"

"Missy," he bites out, like he doesn't want to tell me.

My memory serves me a picture of a tall blonde by Maisy's side at Winterfest. "The blonde."

"Yes." Axel blows out a breath. "I don't want Maisy because Missy is my mate."

The fight leaves me so quickly, I almost stagger. Relief floods me–I don't have to kill Axel for lusting after my mate.

And then the guilt rips into me. What sort of person am I that I would come so close to hurting my own brother?

I take a beat to catch my breath. "How long have you known?"

"Since prom."

"So you've been fighting it, too."

He says nothing. His face is pure misery. I've been there. Just talking about his mate must be torture.

"Say no more."

"Maisy and my friendship is real," he adds then stiffens. Upstairs, Maisy is moving around. I shake off my adrenaline and loosen my stance.

"Guys?" Maisy walks down the stairs, yawning. Her hair is tousled from sleep. I hold out my arm, and to my delight, she comes right to me and tucks herself into my side.

"Hey, Axel," she greets him. "What are you guys talking about?"

"Just planning to get back to Bad Bear," I lie.

"Oh." Her shoulders sag. "All good things must come to an end."

* * *

Maisy

I try to get Axel to stay for breakfast, but he refuses, saying he has to get back to Vegas. "Maisy, will you walk me out?" he asks, and I feel Matthias stiffen. Something's up between them.

Before I can ask what, Matthias releases me. "Go on," he urges although I could've sworn he was reluctant for me to go only a second before. "I'm making omelettes."

"Yum, thank you."

I escort Axel to the door. He won't let me go outside because I'm barefoot, even though I'm warm enough in the blue lounge set and the sunny and 60 degree Vegas January is so much warmer than New Mexico.

"You good?" Axel asks, studying me intently. I noted him staring at my diamond necklace when I was in Matthias' arms. As if he knows it's more than a necklace.

"Yeah," I say. "Better than good." I resist the urge to squirm. I feel like he can see the marks that are under my lounge set.

"Good. If that changes, let me know." He leaves me frowning.

Does he think that he needs to protect me from Matthias? Matthias seems to think so too. It makes me resolve to prove that I can handle him.

"Hey hubby," I return to the kitchen and give Matthias a kiss. "So, we're leaving?"

"Tomorrow. As much as I'd like to keep you here..." he doesn't look happy about heading home, and that makes me feel better.

A spike of anxiety hits me. It'll be good to get back to Bad Bear but what happens between me and Matthias? Will we still be a couple? I mean, we're legally married, and he's giving me sex lessons, but does he have any intention of keeping this up when we get back? Or will it all be over?

"I guess honeymoons don't last."

I wait for him to say it won't be over, but he's all business.

"We need to deal with Lucky Lou and Allen. We're keeping tabs on Lucky Lou. He's searching for your father, too."

"Got it," I say briskly because I'm an adult, and I can handle this. "What will you do when you find him?"

"It's up to you, beautiful."

"I don't know!" I'm flustered. I don't want my dad hurt or in trouble, but I also never want to see him again.

For a moment his eyes flare with a blue light. "Whatever you want, I'll do," he rumbles.

I grab us both coffee and wait for him to serve up the omelettes. "What was that with Axel?" I ask because I don't want any secrets between us. "You both seemed tense."

He puts down his fork, a muscle jerking in his cheek. "I asked him if he was in love with you."

"Axel? With me?"

"Don't sound so surprised. You're a pearl beyond price."

I look away, my eyes smarting. Wow. Okay. Maybe it won't be over when we get back.

"We're just friends," I tell him, touching my diamond

necklace to reassure myself it's there. "We're not really close, but...he always seems to show up at the right time. Just every once in a while, he'll roll up in one of his muscle cars or a bike or whatever he's working on and honk the horn. And he'll take me for a drive." I smile because riding around with Axel was such a nice reprieve from the stress of my life. "We don't even talk much. We just listen to music, or look at the view. It's nice. Not more than a few times a year, but... he seems to know when I'm feeling down." I let out a self-deprecating laugh. "Daisy probably calls him."

"No, I bet he just knows when you need him. He's quiet, but he pays attention."

"He's always been there for me."

"It should've been me," Matthias growls. His eyes flash blue, and I'm learning that's when his bear is coming to the surface. His anger and regret, raw emotion bleeding through. "It should've been me. I never should've stayed away. I missed so much..."

My heart swells.

"I'm here now." I take his hand and rub my finger over the gold band he put on as his wedding ring. He sighs. I feel his regret and understand it. If I had known he had feelings for me, maybe we could have dated even sooner.

But no, I probably wasn't ready. I'm not even sure if I'm ready now. So I take a deep breath and tell him what I really want. "We have one last night in Vegas. Why don't we make the most of it? We could have a night on the town."

"No," he stiffens. "It's not safe."

"Please," I snort. "As if you couldn't keep me safe. C'mon, hubby, you owe me a date. I missed our planned one."

He shakes his head, but I can tell I'm wearing him

down. "I'll let you dress me up any way you like," I singsong. "I'll wear my diamond collar."

His eyes glow blue. I was right–it did mean something.

"And after dinner, we can come back here and spend all night in the playroom. If you wear me out enough, I'll sleep on the flight home."

"This is a bad idea."

I smile because I can see I'm winning. "Please, Matthias. I want the whole world to know that I'm yours."

He groans and slams his chair back then pulls me out of mine into his lap. "All right, wifey. I can't say no to that."

Chapter Seventeen

Matthias

My wife is incandescent when I help her out of the limo and escort her into the Bellagio.

Maybe this wasn't a bad idea. I took as much Moon Cure as my veins would allow. My arm aches, but it's worth it.

Maisy is in an off the shoulder blue gown that matches her eyes. With her long white opera gloves and diamonds sparkling around her neck, she looks like a movie star. People rubberneck as we pass, staring at her as if they're wondering if she's someone famous.

When we stop at the bar by the roulette tables for a drink, I tell her this, and she laughs.

"That's so weird," she wrinkles her nose. "Usually my friend Missy is the one people stare at. She's the glamorous one."

The bartender serves us our drinks. Whiskey for me and pink champagne for her. I let her sip a little and then ask, "How long have you and Missy been friends?"

"Since high school. She was the most popular girl in school."

"Axel has a thing for her," I confide.

"What?" Her forehead wrinkles, then she nods. "I guess I see it. I once thought there was something between them. They both disappeared at prom. I noticed because he was supposed to be my date. And she pretends like she can't stand him, but she mentions him a lot."

"Maybe we should be matchmakers," I murmur. It's fun to conspire with my wife, but I also want to torture Axel a little.

"Like Daisy? We can trap them on the Ferris wheel together."

"Sounds like a plan." I brush a curl back from her face. She's brushed glitter over her cheeks to make them pink and pretty. The color reminds me of her well-fucked pussy.

Does she know that I'm obsessed with her? That there's no other woman for me?

Does she know she's it for me?

I lean in closer. "One more thing. I'm sure Missy is lovely, but I've never noticed her. It's always been you."

* * *

Maisy

Matthias leans on the bar, posing like he's in a photo shoot. In his black tuxedo, he looks like a star of the silver screen. The sort of handsome heartthrob who banters with a tall, regal femme fatale.

I don't feel like I deserve to be on his arm, but he thinks I do, so I keep my shoulders straight.

"High school was hard," I share with him. "Dealing with Allen...my self esteem was a wreck. I was grateful

Missy even noticed me. She's a beauty queen, you know. Her parents made her do all sorts of pageants as a kid. And then she was always the star of our theater productions. I guess I got used to hiding in her shadow."

"No more hiding." He tips my face up to his. "I'm going to show you off to the world."

He kisses me right there in the casino, and then everyone's jaws drop with jealousy. He escorts me with a hand on my back to the Cirque du Soleil theater.

"Do you want to play a little roulette?" he murmurs, but I shake my head. The casino floor is crowded, and the stale smell of cigarette smoke reminds me of Allen.

Matthias' friend who owns the house where we're staying has season tickets that come with VIP perks. They allow us to get into the theater early. We have seats in the balcony right next to the stage. When people start filing in to take their seats, I keep waiting for more people to come and sit in the seats around us, but no one does.

"Is this a private box?" I ask.

"Maybe. Or maybe I bought all the tickets to this balcony, so I could have you all to myself." He stretches out his arm along the back of my seat.

"This is the best date ever," I tell him.

"I have a confession to make. I read your journal when you left it at the clinic. I saw your list of symptoms, and..." He rubs the back of his neck. "I shouldn't have done it, but you were in pain, and I wanted to help."

"It's okay." I put a hand on his knee. "I'm glad you helped me."

"I saw your New Year's resolution list. It fell out of the journal."

I think of my bulleted list. *Glow up, go on a date...* "Oh. Did you read it?"

"Yes."

A hot rush of embarrassment closes my throat. I rub it, wishing I could wipe the flush away. My fingers touch the diamond necklace, and I play with one of the jewels until I can speak. "So when I asked you on a date...is that why you said yes? To help me?" I'm afraid to ask the real question. *Was it a pity date?*

"No." His voice deepens. "Maisy, look at me."

I shake my head a little. I can't. I don't dare to, in case he looks sorry for me.

With a growl he grabs my hand and places it right on his crotch. "Do you feel this?"

My mouth parts in shock. I'm in a gown, he's in a tux, and here he is in the theater, pushing his hard cock into my hand.

"This isn't me helping you," he bites out like he's angry, but I know he's not. Or if he is, he's not angry at me. "This is pure homegrown lust. That's what I feel for you."

I nod, still not able to look at him. He turns to me and pulls me against his chest, so I can hide my hot face against him.

"We're going to work on this," he murmurs, a warrior, picking up a sword to slay my inner demons. "There's no reason for you to think badly of yourself."

"Okay," I whisper. If Matthias wants to be my champion, willing to fight my own insecurities, I'm all for it. Sometimes I need a little help. "Thank you."

"No more negative self-talk, beautiful. I won't allow it."

Yes, daddy. I bite my lip.

In the theater, a few acrobat dancers make their way into the aisles with a little pre-show to entertain us. The main event is going to start soon.

Matthias releases me, so I can compose myself. Once I

wipe the wetness from my eyes, he takes my hand and squeezes it. I can feel him wanting to ask if I'm okay, so I whisper to him, "Where do zombies like to go swimming?"

"The Dead Sea," he whispers back.

I figure that's the end of it, but even when the first act starts, I can feel him watching me.

The show is incredible. I can't tear my eyes away from the synchronized swimming, the contortionists, or the acrobats performing high above the pool, but my nerves are afire, aware of my husband beside me. He's almost vibrating with energy. All his muscles are tense like he's containing the force of his lust.

Halfway through the first act, he slides his hand onto my satin-covered knee. "Spread your legs, little wife."

My pussy throbs, anticipating his touch. I lean back a little, and push my knees apart.

"My good, obedient girl. Keep watching the show."

I fix my eyes on the stage, but my gaze goes hazy as he lifts my skirt and finds a way underneath. At first he's just stroking my knee, then upper thigh, but at a climatic part of the show, when the acrobats are bouncing on a trampoline that sends them thirty feet into the air before they flip into the water, his fingers edge close to my pussy.

My gasp is swallowed by the oohs and ahhs of the crowd.

He brushes my folds and makes a noise when he feels how wet I am.

I get a little reprieve at intermission. He sits back and pulls my dress down. "Do you want anything to eat or drink?"

I shake my head.

"We're having dinner after this, but I wanted something sweet." He licks his fingers.

I duck my head, and he growls, "Don't hide from me. Let me see those blushes. beautiful, I'm obsessed with you."

I rub my arm, mumbling, "I need to lose some weight."

"Absolutely not. I forbid it. I want all of this." He places his huge hand on the swell of my belly. "Soft belly, soft thighs. I'm going to make sure you eat well. Cook for you every night. You're going to eat lots of fruits and vegetables, plus lots of protein and healthy fats. Omega-3s."

"What about my Omega 69s?" I bat my eyelashes at him.

"Can't forget those." He grins. "I'll give you lots of treats. But I know which one will be your favorite."

I glance down at the bulge in his tuxedo pants.

"That's right, beautiful. I eat pineapple regularly."

I perk up at that. "I read that can change the taste of semen. It makes it sweet."

"I'm gonna make sure I taste good for you because you love sucking my cock. Don't you?" Oh, it gets me hot when he slips right into dirty talk in the middle of an ordinary conversation.

I say *yes, sir* even though it's muffled by the finger in my mouth.

"You'll get plenty of exercise, too. Your body is a work of art, and I'm going to admire it properly. And care for it. I'll give you very thorough checkups every single night."

I groan. "Will you wear the glasses?"

"Yes, Maisy, I'll wear the glasses just for you." He sets his hand around my throat again and leans in to kiss me. He smells like expensive cologne, sandalwood and ambergris, with a wild woodsy flavor underneath. My handsome husband. I can hardly believe he's mine.

The second act starts, and he kneels down in front of me. "What are you doing?"

"Do you trust me?"

We're in public. I mean, we're on a balcony, and the lights are down, and no one can really see but... "Yes?"

"I'm going to need a *yes, sir*." He picks up my hand and kisses my knuckles right next to the wedding ring. "If this makes you uncomfortable, I'll sit back in my seat and pretend I didn't order you not to wear panties, so I could have easy access to this sweet pussy."

Oh God. "Yes, sir. Please." I widen my knees.

He pushes up my skirt again. His hot breath hits my folds, and I almost collapse. "I'm going to eat my dessert first. You're not going to come for me until I say. Understand?"

"Yes, sir."

And so the torture begins.

He plays with my pussy, licking it like I'm a bowl of ice cream, and he doesn't have a spoon. I clench my teeth and try not to cry out.

It's only when the final act comes that he lifts his head.

"I don't want you to hold back; you're going to come for me."

Down on stage, the acrobats swan dive a death-defying distance into the pool.

I'm nervous—I don't want to make a scene. I can't pretend that doing this in public doesn't add an edge to the delicious torment.

He lowers his head and licks and licks and licks, pushing me toward the pinnacle. My pleasure crests, and I cry out just as the curtains close and people jump to their feet with a roar of applause.

Chapter Eighteen

Matthias

"That was an amazing show," she says. "I would watch it again every night."

"Me too."

"You didn't even see it."

"What I saw was the most gorgeous sight in the world." And I'm going to see it again. I've decided I'm not letting her go when we get back to Bad Bear. I'm going to make her come every night. I want to worship at the altar of her pussy every morning, and sneak off to have my way with her every day. The way I want her is problematic. It's worse now that I've had a taste. And it's not just sinking my cock and teeth into her. I want to feed her. Bathe her. Carry her, so her perfect toes don't ever have to touch the filthy ground. This cannot be normal. Were my brothers this way with Lana and Paloma?

I just need to strengthen the Moon Cure. I just took a dose before I got in the limo tonight, but it feels like it's already worn off. My limbs feel heavy, but my fangs are slick and ready.

Mate mate mate need need need mark mark mark. My bear is shouting nonstop.

I'm almost out of Moon Cure. But it's fine, I can get more vampire blood, even if I have to fly to Lucius to draw it myself.

She's still breathless as I escort her to a private room in the restaurant overlooking the fountains. We're going to have a candlelight dinner, and then I'm going to end by fucking her on the table while the glowing fountains dance to Debussy. Then I'll take her to the mansion, carry her to the playroom, and test every implement on her sweet ass. I'll have to take more Moon Cure to do it, but fuck it, I'll do it, for her.

Mark mark mark mate mate mate mate.

I ignore my bear, but there's a tremor in my hand as I hold her chair for her like a gentleman.

"Thank you for giving me my date. It was perfect."

"This is just the beginning. We're going to be together. You need to know what I am, who I am first. So when we get back to the mountain, I'll take you on that hike, and I'll show you my bear."

"I'd like that."

Maybe it'll be okay.

"So now that you've seen my New Year's resolution list, I might as well tell you about my plans for the cafe."

"Expansion plans?" I ask, remembering the list.

"Yes, I want to build off the back and side and add a bookstore. I once saw a brewery bookstore, and that inspired me. We'll be a coffee shop with a bookstore by day, and then a coffee shop with a bar by night. I'll host authors for signings and have a space for poetry readings, game nights, and performers like singer/songwriters."

"That sounds amazing."

"I need to pitch it to Daisy and take care of the second mortgage on her house that she took out when I was in high school. All of my paycheck is going there until we get that paid down."

"Maisy, I had no idea you were taking all this on."

"Don't tell Daisy–she doesn't know I'm making extra payments."

"And I've been taking entrepreneurship classes at community college and put together a business plan."

"Do you need investors? You could talk to Lana and Paloma. They've started a foundation that focuses on micro-loans for women-owned businesses."

"Oh...I don't know. I couldn't...they're billionaires!"

"They want their money to do good. They're also serious about investing in their community. They want to raise their kids on the mountain."

"It takes a village."

"Not even a village is enough to handle a set of Bad Bear triplets," I mutter.

Maisy covers my hand with her much smaller one. "You helped raise your brothers. That's why the triplets turned out so well."

"Did they?" In my mind they're still the rambunctious teens who seemed to never grow up.

"Don't be down on yourself. If I'm not allowed, then you aren't either."

"Then yes, raising them was hard. Mom was amazing, but... it was a lot. And then Everest showed up, and he needed a lot of care. I don't think he got enough."

She frowns. "Everest seems like a sweetheart. He's always showing up, wanting to work in the coffeeshop."

"He's refusing to shift out of bear form back to human."

"Yes, well, that has made it difficult. Everest is an adult now, and he gets to make choices. Are there shifter therapists?"

"I'm a shifter doctor, so... probably."

"It doesn't have to be all on you, Matthias," she says gently. "You're a good big brother. An example."

"I tried to be."

"You are. Everyone looks up to you. I don't think anyone works harder for Bad Bear than you. The only time I see you is when you're on your way to the hospital. Or when you're volunteering at the clinic right after a shift. You work too much."

I swallow. I need to tell her that I was working to avoid her...to keep from claiming her. I need to tell her she's my mate.

I don't want her trapped by me before she's ready, before she really understands she's my everything for life. She's only had a taste of how rough I am, and she hasn't even seen my bear. I'm older than her, and she's inexperienced.

"It's been a lot. And...I've never told anyone this, but... my mom was sick, really sick. She doesn't even know how sick. I tried to hide the worst from her, so I didn't scare her."

Maisy's eyes round. "Your mom is sick?"

"She's better now," I say quickly because she looks distressed, and I can't stand to see her upset. "I had to put her into hibernation to slow her body down, so I could cure her. That's why she was asleep for years."

"Oh, my God. That's so intense. Axel never mentioned anything. That's so rough."

"My brothers don't know. I didn't tell anyone."

"So you carried that all alone? Matthias."

My throat closes at the look of compassion she gives me.

She picks up my hand across the table and squeezes it. "That's so awful. So much pressure and responsibility on your shoulders. You should have shared the burden with your brothers. At least with Teddy and Darius–they were old enough to help you handle things."

"They were both gone–Teddy enlisted in the military, and Darius was making his fortune on Wall Street. I didn't want to bother them."

She shakes her head. "What else have you been taking sole responsibility for?"

Keeping away from you. Not marking my fated mate who was far too young and fragile for me.

I open my mouth to confess it all, but the waiter approaches, "Sir, pardon the disruption, but I have a message for you. From your brother."

"Which one?"

The waiter looks panicked, and I wave a hand. "Nevermind. What's the message?"

"I was told to tell you, *Allen alert*."

Fuck. They found Maisy's father.

"He also strongly recommends you turn on your phone."

"Thank you." I pull out my phone and see that I have twenty missed calls and a bunch of texts from all my brothers.

I hit redial on the most recent call. It's Teddy's phone, but Darius answers. "We have Allen. What do you want us to do with him?"

"Great. Where are you?"

"In the party bus, parked in the alley behind the Paris Hotel. I dropped a pin."

"Wait for me. I want to handle him personally." I end

the call and look at Maisy. "Will you excuse me for a moment?"

Maisy grabs my hand. "Wait–no. What is it?"

I hesitate. I don't want to upset her with this. I don't want that man anywhere near his daughter again.

"Handle who? Is it my dad?"

Fuck. I also can't lie to my mate. I nod. "Yes. They've picked him up."

Maisy releases my hand and stands, squaring her shoulders. "I want to speak to him."

I barely contain my bear snarl. My lips curl up, and my fangs lengthen. The idea of my mate in any danger makes me savage. "Not safe." My growl doesn't even sound human.

"No, Matthias," Maisy says firmly. "I need to do this. I need to know why."

The courage in Maisy's tone makes me pay attention. She sounds different. More sure of herself. More grown up.

I nod. "All right." I throw a hundred-dollar bill down on the table to cover our drinks, and we hustle out of the restaurant.

Maisy hikes up her skirts. I lead her out of the restaurant, across the street, and into the alley. We walk away from the people in a construction zone through a boarded up walkway and into the deserted alley beyond.

At the end of the alley, the flashing lights of the party bus signal its presence.

A prickle at the back of my neck puts me on edge. I scent the air for a threat, but this part of town is crowded, so I just smell hundreds of strangers and cigarette smoke. My bear instincts are going off. Maybe I shouldn't have brought Maisy.

I narrow my eyes to peer through the open door of the bus. "Wait here, beautiful," I murmur and climb the steps to crane my neck to see Allen. Teddy gives him a kick in the ribs. The triplets sit on benches around him, scrolling on their phones and eating taffy. Allen's tied up on the floor, bleeding at the mouth and nose like my brothers have worked him over a little already.

"It's okay—" I turn back to get Maisy and freeze, the blood turning to ice in my veins.

A man has Maisy in a headlock with a gun pointed at her temple.

My bear roars with rage, but I somehow manage to remain perfectly still, without shifting to bear form. I'm afraid any sudden movement will get my mate killed.

"You're coming with us," the greasy mobster who dared lay his hands on my mate declares. Two other thugs flank him, also holding pistols. Standing a short distance behind them is Lucky Lou himself—the man I intend to kill just as soon as I get that gun away from my mate's temple. He has a gun trained on me.

My brothers catch on behind me, cursing softly, and drop below window-height.

"You're late for our wedding," Lucky Lou says to Maisy.

Maisy's face has gone pale. Her wide blue gaze locks on mine like she's waiting for instruction. Like she knows I will save her.

Her trust humbles me, and I vow one thousand times over to make sure I earn it by killing everyone of these fuckers.

"She's already married." I use my cool, authoritative doctor voice. "Last time I checked, polygamy was illegal in the state of Nevada."

"She's not married," Lucky Lou insists.

"Yes, I am." Maisy holds up her hand to display her wedding ring. "I got married two days ago."

Lou curses. "I knew that lowlife Dankworth couldn't be trusted. He double-crossed us."

He advances on Maisy, and I jump down the bus steps to land lightly on my feet, my hands in the air like I'm harmless. There's no way in hell I'm letting that man get close to my mate.

"Dankworth didn't," I say smoothly. "I'm the guy who put a wrench in your plans. Maisy is my wife now." I take a step closer to Maisy.

If I can just get her to safety, I can take all of these guys, even with their guns.

"Don't move." Lucky Lou jerks his gun in my direction. "So *you* have my money, then. Well, you're going to sign it over."

"What money?" Maisy asks.

"Your inheritance," Lou snarls.

I can see by the bewildered look on Maisy's face, she doesn't know what he's talking about, either.

"What inheritance?" she asks.

"The one your husband controls as soon as you marry or turn twenty-three. The one owed to me by your asshole father."

So, Maisy receives an inheritance for getting married or after turning twenty-three. That explains the forced marriage. And her birthday is next month, so it seems her father was trying to get control of that money before she did. Allen Dankworth had a trust fund before he partied it all away, so maybe his parents left her something.

Maisy turns a confused face toward the bus, like she wants to ask Allen to explain himself.

Alpha's Mate

"Yeah." Lou waves toward the bus with the butt of his pistol. "Get Dankworth out here, so he can join Maisy's new *husband* in watching me torture her until I get what's mine."

I take one half-step closer to Maisy knowing exactly what will happen the moment Lou's goon steps on the bus.

I ready my bear. I'm shocked I haven't already shifted with our mate in danger, but he must understand when there are guns involved, I need my human brain at top function for strategy. I keep my gaze trained on the gun at Maisy's temple and count down in my head. Three...two...one.

The party bus shakes with a six-bear roar.

The guy holding Maisy jerks his gaze in the direction of the rocking bus where a man screams.

I leap, shifting mid-air, slamming the gun to the ground with a giant bear paw.

I take a bullet in the shoulder from Lou as he yells, "Get the girl! Don't let her get away!"

Maisy doesn't let out a peep. She enacts what looks like a practiced self-defense move, breaking the pinky finger of the guy still holding her in a headlock, squirming out from his grasp, and stomping on the side of his knee to cripple him.

I tear his head off with one mighty swipe of my paw and throw it at Lou, who, based on his horrified expression, caught up to the fact that I'm no longer human. I'm a bear wearing the shredded clothes of a man, and I'm out for blood.

I pick up my mate by the waist, shielding her body by gently tossing her over the hood of the bus as Lou empties his chamber in my back. She understands, rolling and sliding across it to duck behind the other side in safety.

183

My brothers burst from the bus, spilling out into the alley with roars. I lift my snout to the sky and roar, giving my bear free rein. The scent of blood and urine from the terrified thugs reaches my nostrils. My brothers seem to understand the kills belong to me because they catch and release, toying with the men, making a game of it until I end every single one of them with my claws through their hearts, their heads severed from their bodies, and their blood soaking the pavement.

"It's over." Teddy drops a hand on my shoulder. He's back in human form.

I roar, wanting to kill them all over again.

They. Touched. My. Mate.

"I know," he says, as if he heard my bear's rant. "But your mate needs you now. Shift back, brother."

My mate...needs me now.

My mate! I whip my head around to find Maisy.

"Matthias?" She emerges from behind the bus.

I instantly shift back. "Maisy!"

Canyon hands me a towel, and I use it to wipe the worst of the blood off my face and hands as I jog to her.

Fate, I hope she's not afraid of me now.

"Maisy, are you okay?"

She barrels straight into my arms. Thank fuck. "Maisy. You were so brave." I stand and rock her, swaying from side to side like she needs soothing. Really, I'm the one who needs soothing. I need to hold my mate. Know she's safe. Reassure myself.

My bear still wants blood. I don't know if I'll ever get over seeing a gun pointed at her head. If anyone touches my wife, they won't be long for this Earth.

"Where did you learn those moves?" I ask, trying to

sound normal. Like I didn't just turn into a beast and execute four men in front of her.

She lets out a puff of laughter. "I took a self-defense class." She tips her face up to mine. "What's a martial artist's favorite beverage?"

I can guess the answer, but I let her tell me. "What?"

"Kara-tea!"

Chapter Nineteen

Maisy

"Let me see you." Matthias carries me from the party bus inside the mansion.

After he ripped Lucky Lou and his men apart, he bustled me inside the party bus while his brothers made quick work of cleaning up the scene.

Teddy said they would spread the word that it was a drug deal gone bad. Axel said someone named Kylie would plant texts on Lucky Lou's phone to point to an active branch of the cartel in this area to give the authorities a trail.

Allen was on the bus, shaking and freaking out because he'd seen men turn into bears. He'd peed his pants. It was disgusting. I realized there was nothing more I ever wanted from him. I didn't need to have a relationship. Didn't need to believe he cared.

I just. Don't. Care.

What a relief. My pathetic relationship with him has clouded my entire life. It feels great to have it over.

Matthias asked how I'd like them to handle him, and I said I didn't want to see him again. Ever.

"If that's what you want, beautiful, consider it done. He doesn't get to breathe your air," Matthias said.

I heard Teddy tell Matthias he'd need to have his mind wiped. I don't know exactly what that means, but I added, "Can you make sure...he doesn't hurt anyone anymore?"

Matthias had nodded. "We can make that happen."

He carries me into the en suite bathroom and gently sets me on my feet on the floor. We're both covered in blood. He turns on the shower.

"I need to examine you. If he left one fucking bruise..."

"You'll tear his head off?" I try to make light of it by quirking my eyebrow up because if I don't, I'll probably hyperventilate.

I just saw seven grown men turn into bears and rip Lucky Lou and his men to shreds.

He rubs his face. "I'm so sorry you saw that, Maisy."

"No, it's okay. I knew you'd protect me, and you did."

Matthias kisses my forehead and turns me gently to unzip my dress. It falls to a puddle at my feet. He unhooks my strapless bra, and it tumbles off, too.

He shucks the sweats one of his brothers gave him after he shifted. Then, he picks me up with his forearm under my ass, lifting me to straddle his waist. I'm a big girl–full-bodied–but he makes me feel tiny.

He steps into the shower still holding me and turns slowly, letting the spray of water shower both of us. He turns us around and around until the water runs clear, and the blood is gone.

"Are you going to put me down?" I laugh.

"I don't want to." His voice is gruff with emotion.

I inhale the steamy air and hold my breath. It feels significant that after a lifetime of worrying I was unloveable I'm suddenly married to a man who cares deeply. It's strange and incredible, but it must be true. Here I am, in his arms. Feeling loved. Protected. Cherished.

How did we get here in just a few short days?

I almost want to pinch myself to see if it's all a dream. Maybe I'm still drugged, bouncing around in the back of a rape van, and I never woke up in Vegas. Never got married to the man of my dreams. Never had my first kiss. Gave my first blowjob. Had my mind blown with orgasms.

But nothing has ever felt so real.

"I want to have sex with you," I tell him.

Matthias pins me against the shower wall, still not lowering me to my feet, and kisses my breast. "We've been having sex." His voice is impossibly deep and gravelly.

"I want you to take my virginity."

He emits a bear growl. His teeth lengthen and eyes glow electric blue.

My nipples tighten into hard buds. The place where my bare pussy rubs against his belly grows even more slick. His cock lengthens, lifting to touch my ass.

"What are you waiting for?" I know I'm taunting him. It's on purpose. I don't need to be treated with kid gloves.

He lets out another growl. My bear daddy is losing it.

I love it.

He kicks off the water with his foot and steps out of the shower. I lick the water droplets from his neck, then give him a love bite.

He roars.

Wow. He grabs a towel and carries me into the bedroom. We crash onto the bed with him on top of me, his open mouth dragging over my breast as his hips settle right into the cradle of my legs. I feel the long ridge of his cock nested right against my pussy. I rock my hips to rub against it, and Matthias groans.

This is it. I'm going to have sex. Well, like he said, we've had sex, but I'm going to experience penetration.

D in V.

The whole thing. My first time with the man of my dreams, just as I always imagined it.

I reach between our bodies to hold his cock. His growl would scare me except I know he likes it. I can tell by the way his cock surges in my hand, thickening and lengthening.

I direct it toward my entrance.

Matthias seems like he's trying to speak, but all I hear are growls. I smile and pull him toward me. He seems to lose control, shoving deep.

I cry out at the mingled pain and pleasure, and Matthias instantly stops, his glowing eyes wide with alarm.

I don't want him to stop. I love the sensation, just like I love when he spanks me. I rock my hips to move him inside me.

He seems to gather control, slowly gliding in and out of me as he returns his attention to his mouth on my nipple.

"Ooh!" I cry out when Matthias' canine scrapes my nipple.

He rears his head back like he's afraid of hurting me. His fangs are nearly as long as they were when he was in bear form.

I practically soak the bed as my body reacts with pure lust.

Matthias' nostrils flare—a reaction I now realize must be him taking in my scent. He shoves into me a little harder. A little faster.

I let him know with my moans how much I like it. I touch my own breasts, cupping them and squeezing them.

My lover goes wild, like seeing me in the throes of pleasure sends him into orbit. He pounds into me harder. The bed slams against the wall. I now understand why he was afraid of hurting me, but it doesn't hurt. He's rough, he's carnal, but it's all wonderful.

I'm able to take him deeper as my body adjusts to his size. I'm sopping wet and slick, and he glides in and out like my body was made for him. It feels so delicious.

I don't believe anything could feel better than this.

"Yes! Yes, Matthias!" I cry out.

Matthias' fangs gleam white against his dark skin. The room spins. My eyes roll back in my head.

Somehow, I remember to ask for permission. "Sir, I need to come! May I please come?"

"Come!" he roars. He stands on his knees and lifts my legs, so my ankles hang over his shoulders. He grips the tops of my thighs, lifting my ass off the bed. His loins slap against my ass in a jackhammer motion as he fucks me fast and hard.

Oh. My. Gawd. It's so good. So good. So–

I scream as the orgasm rolls over me. My internal muscles pulse and release.

Matthias doesn't stop; he continues to plow into me as he lowers my ass to the bed and leans forward, so I'm in a plow position, practically folded in half. Only then does he slow, breathing in a deep rhythmic pattern like he's trying to calm himself. Trying to get control.

I don't want him in control. I want him to come with me.

I deliberately squeeze my muscles around his cock.

He lets out a surprised shout.

I do it again, and his panting breath comes faster.

"Maisy!" He sounds alarmed. Suddenly he's pounding into me again, his face contorting with pleasure. He shoves in deep and groans, and I swear I feel the heat of his cum spilling inside me as his hips jerk and buck.

His teeth graze my shoulder. I gasp, my loose muscles jerking to attention when he nearly breaks the skin.

Matthias rears his head back, alarm scrawled across his face. He pulls out and backs up off the bed.

My hand flies to the place his canines scraped. He didn't break the skin; he just bit a little harder than I expected. It's fine. I might have a tiny bruise there. No big deal.

But Matthias seems horrified. He tries to say something, but it only sounds like growls. He holds one finger up and rushes out the door.

What...the hell?

I don't need medical attention, if that's what he's thinking.

"I'm okay, Matthias!" I call after him to put his mind at ease. "Totally fine! Come back!"

When he doesn't answer, I roll out of bed and get up to follow. Foolish man. He's ruining the moment by treating me like I'm breakable.

I'm going to tell him that.

I find him in the kitchen, with his doctor's kit dumped on the counter. He's jabbed a syringe with a dark fluid into his arm. A tight band of rubber constricts the blood vessels on his arm to make them stand out.

"Matthias?" I stare in shock.

I'm instantly sick. Memories of watching my parents shoot up in my early childhood flood my brain. I feel dizzy.

His expression wears dismay.

He's an addict?

Like my parents? What is this? Oh God, did he somehow know about my trust fund? Does he need the money for drugs? Or a gambling addiction? I think back to the past few days. The diamond jewelry. The "friend's" mansion. The box seats and Cirque. What kind of small town doctor has friends like that?

I watch as his elongated teeth recede. The electric blue fades from his warm brown eyes.

"Maisy, I'm sorry, I'm under control now."

"Wh-what are you doing?" My voice must hold a mountain of disgust because I watch understanding dawn in his expression. His forehead wrinkles, his eyes appear regretful. "Oh sweetheart. This looks bad to you, doesn't it?"

I can't speak. Can't move. I'm rooted to the spot.

"It's just medicine to control my bear. It's to keep me from claiming you."

Ice sluices through my veins. I don't know what he means, but I don't like it.

I don't like any of this.

"What?"

"You're my mate, Maisy. I have to take Moon Cure to keep from claiming you."

Chapter Twenty

Matthias

Fuck.

I couldn't have fucked this any more.

I almost lost control and marked Maisy back there. And now she's seen me injecting myself with Moon Cure.

It must've triggered her childhood trauma because my lovely mate looks like she wants to run as fast and far as she can away from me.

She stumbles back, and I dive forward to steady her.

"Don't," she snaps, shaking my hands off her forearms. Her face is pale. "Let go. I don't know what's going on, but I don't like it."

"I can understand that, Maisy. I totally can. I'm sure with your parents–"

"What did you mean by *keep from claiming* me?"

I want to scoop Maisy up in my arms and carry her back to the bedroom, but I can tell she's not interested in my comfort right now. She wants an explanation.

I yank the band off my arm and deposit the needles in

the sharps container. "Come—let's sit down. I can explain the biology of mates."

Maisy stalks back into the bedroom, but instead of sitting down, she pulls on clothes, like she's feeling vulnerable and needs to cover up.

Shifters aren't shy about being naked, but—so it's not weird—I also yank the sweatpants that my brothers had on the party bus back on.

"Have a seat," I invite.

"No, I'm good." She folds her arms across her chest.

This really isn't going well. The needle must've been more triggering than I even imagined. She must think I'm a junkie or an addict. But she has it wrong. I do have an addiction—but it's not to a drug. I'm addicted to her. The Moon Cure is to treat that vice.

"According to the lore, every shifter has one true mate. Supposedly, it's orchestrated by fate. As a scientist, I hypothesize that it's actually related to biology."

Maisy stares at me without reaction, so I plunge on. Science is my go-to when things get tough. I studied medicine after my parents' death as a means to control my surroundings when things felt out of control. When Winnie, our adoptive mother, grew sick, I was grateful I understood the biology beneath her illness, so I could save her. Then, when I found my fated mate lived in my small town and was far too young for me, I developed Moon Cure to keep my bear in check.

Once Maisy hears the science behind our connection, she'll understand everything.

"Shifters know their 'fated mate'"--I use air quotes around the phrase *fated mate*— "by scent. Because there's only one mate per shifter, and yours could be anywhere on the planet, only about one in twenty shifters find their mates although I'd like to set up a survey and compile the data from the last twenty years because that number may be changing. Another thing that has changed in the last ten years is a surge in the number of fated mates with humans." I indicate her with my open palm.

Her lips tighten into a thin line. She takes a step backward, like she wants more space between us which doesn't make sense.

"Once a male shifter finds his fated mate, he will mark her, permanently embedding his scent into her skin through a mating bite to let other males know she's taken."

Maisy's fingers drift to the place I nearly marked her, and she rubs the skin there.

"In order to increase the chances of finding your fated mate, shifters attend mating games around the world. The chances of me finding my fated mate in the same small town where I live must be miniscule, and yet, there you were." I extend my palm to her again with a smile, but she doesn't smile back.

"If a male shifter finds his mate but doesn't claim her, or if an alpha shifter never finds and marks a mate, he can go moon mad. Basically, he turns feral, unable to shift from his animal form back to human form. When that happens, they have to be put down for the safety of both the shifter and human communities."

Maisy still doesn't speak, so I plow on. "I developed Moon Cure to treat the onset of moon madness. I use vampire blood."

"Vampires?" She blinks. I guess she doesn't know about vampires yet.

"Yes, but never mind about that. The point is, I am only taking this medicine to prevent hurting you."

"You'd never hurt me."

"But I want to. I want to mark you."

"So..." Maisy seems to work to swallow, "You developed Moon Cure, so you wouldn't mark me?"

I smile at her. She *does* understand. "Exactly."

"Because you didn't want to mate me."

I frown, suddenly hating the direction this is going. "No. Because you were too young. Maisy, you were only fifteen when you hit puberty, and I realized you were my mate. Claiming you would've been wrong in every way."

Her lips part in shock. Her face turns white. She steps back, like I've struck her.

What did I do?

I reach for her, and she steps back again. "I need a moment."

* * *

Maisy

My mind spins out, unable to even process what's happening. I walk back out to the kitchen where Matthias' medical bag still sits on the kitchen counter as a sordid reminder. He's been *shooting up* to keep from claiming me.

Taking *drugs*.

I'm cold and clammy. My heart pounds, and a sick feeling twists in my gut.

On some level, I recognize that some of this–the initial upset–is related to childhood trauma. My nervous system is in fight or flight because I saw Matthias in the same position I found my mom before she died.

But there's more to it than that. I feel so...unwanted. I can't tell if my sense of rejection is logical–all I know is that I feel it in every cell of my body.

I just need some space to sort through my thoughts. Unfortunately, Matthias follows me into the kitchen.

"Maisy, beautiful, please. Let me hold you," he pleads behind me.

I turn and swallow. "Let me get this straight," my voice is quiet. "You've been taking a drug to keep from claiming me?"

He nods warily. "But if it bothers you, I'll stop. I understand how upsetting it must be to you."

"For *seven years*?"

To his credit, Matthias looks miserable. I know he didn't mean to hurt me, but he has.

Deeply.

He spreads his hands. "I tried to stay away from you, Maisy. You were far too young for me. I knew how flustered I made you–I presumed it was because you could feel our biological connection, and it confused you since I was so much older."

He knew how *flustered*...

Ugh. Humiliation washes through me as memories of how I spilled coffee, stammered, and became tongue-tied every time he walked into the cafe. The whole time, he was thinking of me as a child. Someone "far too young" with whom he has an inconvenient biological connection.

So basically, he wasn't interested in *me* as a person. Of course he wasn't! Why would he be–I was a nobody. But his animal body has an attraction to my physical body.

And apparently, what I thought was some kind of deep soul connection was also just biology. I was never in love with Dr. Hunk. It was my body. I had no choice in the matter.

I don't like this.

What felt like a magical, mystical, true love has now been reduced to an unwanted biological urge.

Ugh!

It makes me feel unwanted and worthless.

"Our *biological connection*," I repeat hollowly. My stomach twists up again in a painful knot.

"Yes."

I blink rapidly, and tears spear my eyes.

Matthias looks horrified. "What did I say, Maisy? Why does that upset you?" He comes closer and reaches for me.

"Don't." I hold up a hand. "Don't come near me. I–" I shake my head to arrange my thoughts. "I need to go home."

"Why?" He steps closer again, and I move away. "Maisy, what's bothering you? Talk to me, please."

The part of me that wants to fight back surfaces, and I pin him with a blazing look. "Yes, Matthias," I snap. "You flustered me. I guess I did feel the *biological* connection between us."

He appears confused. "Why is that upsetting? What am I missing, Maisy?"

"Nothing. Nothing at all. I'm glad you found a way to control your *biological* attraction to me. I would hate for you to have to give in and actually, you know, mate with someone you didn't want. Someone so much *younger* and easily flustered."

"Maisy, beautiful. I didn't mean to offend you. I didn't mean it that way."

Tears spill down my cheeks. "I don't know how else to take it. Basically, the only reason you're here is because your biology demands it. If it were up to you–to your head and your heart–you wouldn't even be with me."

"No. That's not true."

"It *is* true. You just took a drug to keep yourself from

mating me." I wave a hand in the direction of his doctor bag. "Clearly, you don't think we're right for each other. You've avoided me for *seven years.* I've been an adult for four of those, but you never made contact. You didn't show up until I was in danger. And then, it was probably because your biology forced you to. So don't worry. I'll keep my distance from you, so you don't have to keep poisoning yourself with drugs to keep from claiming me."

I pick up his phone from the counter and turn the screen to his face to unlock it, then dial up Axel.

"I'm going back to Bad Bear. I'd appreciate it if you didn't contact me." I hold my head high.

Matthias may think of me as a little flustered girl, but he's the one who missed out. I'm all woman. We can chalk my inexperience up to biology–I guess some part of me was confused and waiting for him, but that's over.

I'm a grown woman, and if I'm not enough for him, it's his damn loss.

Chapter Twenty-One

Maisy

I cling to my resolve to be strong and bottle it all up and wait until I'm home before I lose it.

After calling Axel, he got us both on the next commercial flight to Albuquerque, and then rented a car and drove us back to Bad Bear. I didn't say a word the whole way, and neither did he.

Thank God for friends like him.

Daisy is waiting on the doorstep. I run to her, and she opens her arms wide, like she used to when I was little. I hug her carefully because she feels so thin and frail in my arms. This time, I'm holding her up, instead of the other way around.

"Maisy," her voice is clogged with tears. "Thank goodness you've returned."

"I'm here. I'm okay." She's shaking, and I'm afraid she might be cold standing on this icy stoop. "Let's get inside."

She lifts her head, and her face is wet as she looks

around. Axel's already driven off, probably to give me space. "Where's Matthias? I want to thank him for bringing you back to me."

I try to be strong, but my face crumples a bit, and Daisy realizes something is wrong.

"Oh no, sweetheart. Tell me everything."

* * *

Maisy

"So that's why I came home early," I tell Missy. She was still at her mom's in Santa Fe and dropped everything to come up the mountain for a sleepover tonight. My throat is scratchy from explaining everything while holding back tears. I cried a bunch when telling Daisy, but with Missy, I leave out the shifter stuff, so all she knows is that I found out Matthias was with me because he felt obligated. "He doesn't want me, he just felt like he needed to help me. Like a protective big brother."

"Oh, Maisy." Missy sets her mug of hot chocolate on my bedside table and scoots closer, so she can take my hand. "I'm sure that's not true. He said yes to the date."

"Only because he found my New Year's resolution list and thought he was helping me," I whisper. I can't cry, I have no more tears. My tear ducts ache. There's a black hole in the pit of my stomach.

I felt strong when I marched away from Matthias, clinging to my pride, but now, with my best friend, I allow myself to wallow. I deserve a damn pity party.

"I just feel like no one's chosen me. Not my father, not my mother. I even had a pity date to the prom."

"I chose you. Daisy chose you." She squeezes my hand.

I look out the window. It's snowing again. The whole world has darkened even though it's not yet dusk.

"Daisy had no choice. She took me in because she had to–my mom O.D'ed, and my dad was a drug addict, too. And you're an amazing best friend, but...I don't know. Sometimes I feel like I'm just your sidekick." I don't know why all my truths are tumbling out right now. I don't want to hurt Missy, but I just can't hold it in.

I guess I'm just too demoralized to pretend things are fine with me when they're not.

Missy looks dismayed.

"It's not your fault. I'm not blaming you. But you're the pretty one. The popular one."

Missy looks shocked. "You're nuts. First of all, Daisy adores you. You've never been a burden on her. I've always been jealous of how much she loves you. And I'm so sorry you feel that way about us. You're the only person who has been a true friend to me. When we met at school, you were the *only* one who didn't hate me for being Miss New Mexico Teen at fourteen–a pageant I never wanted to enter but had to because my mom's love is conditional, by the way."

It's true that other girls hated Missy, but I didn't even know she'd noticed. She always acted so confident. But of course, she's a great actress.

I give her a hug. "I'm sorry your mom sucks."

She squeezes me tight. "I'm sorry yours died. And I know you're hurting, but it's not true that you're unwanted. We love you for *you*. Because you're awesome."

"Thanks." We pull apart, and I wipe my tears.

I don't feel awesome. I feel like I'm still that little girl who was excited for her dad to visit only to realize he just wanted her birthday money.

I got duped. I thought I meant something to Matthias, but it turned out it was just biology. He didn't want me. He was taking drugs to resist me.

Ugh.

Matthias is back on the mountain with his brothers. Daisy called Winnie to confirm. I told him not to contact me, so it's stupid that I'm hurt he hasn't come to see me.

Do I want him to fight for me?

Yeah, I guess I do.

But I don't know what he could say to change the hurt I feel.

He was doing everything he could to keep from biting me and making it permanent.

He wanted to protect me, but...he was leading me on. This was worse than a pity fuck. I thought it was real.

He fucking *married* me. And let me joke about having a honeymoon and helped me with my virginity, and...oh God, it felt so real. I mean I guess it was real, but just the physical part. Just frickin' *biology*.

Missy squeezes my hand. "You're going to get through this. And you'll get over him. You've been through a lot in the past few days, but you've lived through worse. You got this."

"Thanks." I don't feel like I am living. I feel like I'm the dirt on someone's shoe.

Missy forces a smile. "Why did the dad stop using his discount card to scrape his windshield?"

"He only got ten percent off," I answer dully. Not even dad jokes can cheer me up. I cringe at all the times I told them to Matthias like a big, goofy idiot. Probably another instance where he thought I was too young.

No wonder he doesn't want me as a wife.

"I'll get us more hot cocoa," Missy says. She gives my hand one more squeeze and heads out into the hall, where I hear murmured voices. She and Daisy are conferring.

My phone beeps, and I check it. For a second, I wonder if it's Matthias reaching out, but no, it's a text from Axel. It loads slowly, and when it appears it takes my breath away.

It's our wedding photo. We're at the aisle of the little chapel, the triplets laughing in the background, in their kilts and purple bouquets.

Matthias and I look so happy. I look like a freaking movie star. The star of the show.

I was so happy–even after being kidnapped to marry a mobster by my own dad. I touch my face. Was that really me?

I was glowing. Not just from the diamonds around my neck. I'm in love.

Matthias looks happy too. But it must have been a lie.

Missy returns to find me sobbing.

"What happened? Who do I need to kill?" Her fierce tone reminds me why she's my best friend.

Wordless, I show her the photo. Her little "Oh," makes me cry harder. Because she gets it. She puts her arms around me and lets me soak her sweatshirt with my tears.

"I wanted it," I tell her. I had it, and I lost it. And I want it back, even if it was all fake.

I press my face into Missy's shoulder. My belly cramps with familiar pain, but it's not the ovarian cysts acting up.

It's heartbreak.

* * *

Matthias

I stare at the charred log in my fireplace. It'll be cold tonight, well below freezing. I should light a fire, but I don't feel like it.

The cold numbs me the way the Moon Cure did. It's about the only relief I'll ever get, far more than I deserve.

Maisy. Maisy. Maisy. My bear won't stop chanting her name. As if I were thinking of anyone or anything else.

I hurt Maisy. After all these years of trying to hold back to avoid exactly that, I never saw that it would be my act of holding back that inflicted the deepest wound.

A distant crunch of a boot alerts me to a visitor. Axel opens my door and slips inside without asking permission. He takes in the sight of me staring at the empty fireplace. I don't look up, don't move. I don't have the energy.

On the bright side, I don't want to kill him anymore. He's the only tie I have to Maisy right now. He'll take care of her in the way I can't.

"Have you talked to Maisy?" he asks.

Just hearing her name sends a wave of fresh pain throbbing through me. I shake my head, feeling too tired to speak.

"I wanted to give you this." Axel sets something on my coffee table with a click. It's the diamond necklace. Her collar. "She left it in my car."

Of course she did. Why would she keep it? "What about the ring?"

"I didn't see it."

I'm still wearing mine. I realize I'm twisting the gold band around my finger and drop my hands. "Is she okay?"

"I think you know the answer to that."

She's broken-hearted. I sold her a fairy tale and shattered it. There's no going back. She knows the sort of person I am now.

This is for the best.

I swallow around the lump in my throat. "I'm going to need you to watch over her."

"That's your job." His eyes glitter with his bear. He's pissed at me, and I get it. I'm pissed at myself.

"Not anymore." My bear grumbles, and I lose myself in the lonely sound. "She asked me not to contact her."

Axel steps in front of me, snapping his fingers to get my attention. "I don't know what happened between you two, but you have a responsibility to her. You married her. Why in the hell haven't you marked her yet?"

"What was I supposed to do?" I thunder, all my frustrations suddenly flooding to the surface, especially because Axel seems to be demanding the same thing Maisy was. "Mark a girl who'd never been kissed before our wedding night? How fair is that to her? I'm ten years older than her, Axel. She'd never been on a single date before. Never been kissed. Still lives at home with her grandmother. You think it's right for me to snatch her up and mark her just because it's what *I* need? What about her needs?"

Axel shakes his head. "She's a grown woman. Did you give her a choice?"

I grip the sides of my chair. "I'm protecting her!" I'm full-on shouting now, which I never do. I'm the one in the family who never loses his temper. Who is always cool, calm, and controlled. Now I can't even think with my bear caterwauling at me to find Maisy.

"You're not protecting her. You're protecting yourself." Axel shakes his head. "If you leave her alone, you're not the man I thought you were."

"What do you want me to do?" I snarl. "She asked me not to contact her."

"I want you to be worthy of her."

I say nothing. *I'm not. I never was.*

Axel shakes his head and walks to the door. He opens it and turns to look at me. "Get your head out of your ass, Matthias. Maisy needs you, whether she admits it or not."

It's a full bear-roar that comes out of my throat as he shuts the door. I shove up from the chair and pace the room, considering Axel's words.

He might be right, but I'm not going to railroad her into this mating. It's the one thing I promised myself from the start. Maybe it's how I got myself into this mess, but I have integrity. I will keep this vow.

For her.

Maisy Maisy Maisy—

I'm losing control, and I don't know what to do.

The memory of her innocent New Year's resolution list scrawled in neat, hopeful writing flashes in my mind:

> Glow up
> Dr. appointment for PCOS
> Plan DD expansion
> Set boundaries with Allen
> Stand up for yourself!!! You can do it!
> Go on a date

My eyes burn as I let out a bitter laugh. Well, my sweet, beautiful mate completed all of them, including standing up for herself.

Good for her.

Maybe I should make a New Year's resolution list.

I grab a sheet of paper. My fingers have long, curved claws—my bear taking over. It takes me a few tries to get them to retract. Finally, I grab a big, black, permanent marker and hold it in my palm to write. My scrawl fills the whole page, but that's okay. I only need to write out one thing:

Get Maisy back.

Chapter Twenty-Two

Maisy

After a restless night, I wake up at five am.

Like it's an ordinary day in an ordinary week, and my biggest problems are getting to the cafe on time to prep before opening.

Like I didn't just get married last week and have my heart broken in Vegas.

I've laid low for a few days, bed-rotting and watching holiday movies with Missy, but now I need to get back to some form of normalcy. So I get up and get ready for work. I can help prep and then hide in the back once Jenny comes in to run the morning shift with one of our part-timers.

Valentine's day is coming up, and normally I'd be planning all sorts of themed drinks and hauling out our heart-and-daisy-chain decorations to give the cafe's seating area a pop of red, but this year, I wish I could hit a button and disappear the entire holiday. For everyone.

Maybe I should take Missy up on her offer and move to L.A. I'd have to start over, but working mindless hours might help me forget Matthias.

Who am I kidding? I'll never forget this.

My time with him was the happiest of my life. What hurts is that it wasn't real.

I walk down the snowy road to the cafe, crunching the ice beneath my boots. The cold nips at my nose and the tips of my ears. In the pre-dawn dark, the snow seems to glow.

There's a rustling in the woods by me, and I stop and peer through the leaves. Is someone there?

But no, it's probably just a wild animal. A fox, a squirrel. This early, no one's out. No one except a certain young doctor, returning from a hospital shift...No, I'm not going to think about him.

The bell over the door jingles when I enter the cafe. Normally the daisy-themed decor would cheer me up, but right now, it's too bright. Too much.

I head right to the back and get to work pulling stuff out of the freezer, turning on the oven and pulling the sheets of scones out of the refrigerator that Ryan prepped the night before, so Jenny can bake them in the morning.

The front door jingles, and someone calls, "Maisy?"

I frown. It's too early for Jenny to be in, and that sounded like my grandmother.

It is Daisy. She's at the front door, stomping her boots on the mat to shake the snow off them. Then she heads right to the thermostat and cranks it up.

"What are you doing here?"

Daisy isn't a morning person, and she hasn't covered a dawn shift in years. I made a point of taking over this as soon as she trusted me with opening on my own.

"Good morning. Good to see you up and about." She gives me a smile that softens her brisk tone. She wanted me to take time off, so I shouldn't feel guilty about wallowing for the past few days. "I texted Jenny yesterday and gave her the morning off. Figured she could use a break since she's been covering for you, and you do the work of six people."

"I don't—"

"You do. It's time we all recognized that. Come here." She heads to the office, beckoning me to follow her. "I have something to show you."

I trail behind her. Even though I've slept a lot these past few days, I feel foggy. I need some cold brew before I can match even half of Daisy's energy.

The cafe office is tiny. I try to keep the place neat, but there's always stacks of paperwork, payment stubs and tax forms and glossy brochures from our suppliers overloading the desk. Daisy takes the chair behind the desk and motions me to sit in the only remaining one.

"This is a long time coming." Daisy starts clearing papers, stacking them into piles. I should stop her—she just mixed some employee W-2s with our quarterly tax filing. She actually seems nervous. "I should've done it years ago. I should've...well, never mind. If anything, the past few days have been a wake up call."

I frown, trying to figure out what she's talking about. My brain can't keep up with this conversation.

She lays a leather bound folio between us. "This is for you."

I make no move to take it. "What is it?"

"My last will and testament. You're my beneficiary, of course—"

I'm shaking my head. "No, we don't need to talk about this."

"Maisy, we do. When I realized you were gone." Her voice catches, and her eyes take on a haunted look, "well, I realized just how much I've been taking for granted. How much I lean on you. No," —she holds up a hand— "listen to me. I'm ninety-two. I don't have time to beat around the bush." She flips open the folio and hands me something. It's her mortgage statement.

"I just found out that you've been making extra payments on the mortgage. You didn't have to do that, Maisy."

"I wanted to help," I say.

"I don't know how I got so lucky to have a grand-daughter like you," Daisy says.

I tear up.

"What I really want to do right now is this." Daisy hands me a piece of paper.

I skim it but can't comprehend the legalese. *Daisy Day Cafe owner split.* And my full name, *Daisy May Bennett.*

"As of today, you are a co-owner of the cafe. Fifty-fifty. Now, I know you work here a lot more than me, but I'm willing to sign off on anything you want to do..." She keeps talking, but I can't hear her.

I set the paper down. I'm breathing hard. "You're not dying."

"I hope not. But we never know how long we have. And the one thing I promised when you were gone–" her voice wavers again—"was to make sure you knew how important you are to me. To this town."

I look from her to the paper and back down again. I don't know what to think. A few minutes ago, I was thinking of escaping town forever.

"Maisy, I know you're going through it. And I know it's hard. I just want you to know...you are everything to me. I want you to know that I wouldn't still be alive if it weren't for you. You keep me young. You give me purpose. You light up my life."

Tears spring into my eyes. "Thank you. I'm so grateful you became my guardian after–"

Daisy cuts me off. "I should've taken guardianship of you sooner. Before your mom died." Her voice clogs, and her eyes swim. "I knew she and your dad were using, but I wasn't sure how bad it was."

I reach across the desk and pick up her thin, papery hand. "You couldn't have known." Poor Daisy. I know she'll never get over losing her only daughter to drugs. Losing my mom was rough, but I was so young. And I had Daisy.

Oh. I guess she's telling me she feels the same way.

"If you'd had a normal life, you would've moved out after high school. I know you stayed in Bad Bear because of me." Daisy chokes up again.

I rise to my feet and make my way around the desk to her. She stands, so we can hug. She's smaller than me, yes, but so strong. It's a relief to be in her arms and have her here for me to hug. *I'll never take this for granted,* I tell myself. *Never.* For a moment we just hold each other.

"Well." Daisy lets me go and dabs at her eyes. I've rarely seen her cry. She's like a soldier, stoically forging on, but doing that for decades comes at a cost. "That's that. Half the cafe is yours. And if you want to take off and leave, well, we'll hire some people and eventually be able to send you owner's profits to wherever you go–"

"I'm not leaving," I say. "I'm staying." As soon as I say it, I know it's true. I'm still a wreck, I still have a broken heart, but I love Bad Bear. And I have big plans for the cafe.

"Okay, good. Whatever you want to do."

"Actually, there are some things I'd like to do for the cafe. I want to expand. I even made a business plan..." I trail off as I realize something.

"What? What is it?"

"I just was going to say, we don't have the money to do it now. But we might. I might." And I start laughing. The inheritance Allen wanted to get so badly. It's mine. I guess technically Matthias controls it, but he won't stand in my way.

Maybe it's time I claim what belongs to me.

Chapter Twenty-Three

atthias

Maisy Maisy Maisy—

I stand in bear form in the woods on the edge of town, staring at the Daisy Day Cafe.

I haven't slept in five days. Haven't been in human form in as long, either. I stay up all night watching Maisy through her window. I followed her to the cafe, keeping to the forest, so she couldn't see me. I shouldn't let myself be seen in bear form, even if half the town knows what I am.

The trouble is, I can't stay away from Maisy.

Even now, I'm waiting for her to come to the front door to unlock it for the day. Maybe I'll get a glimpse of her sweet smile as she greets her regulars.

Maisy Maisy Maisy—

I catch the scent of my brothers in the wind. Everest is nearby. He smells like bees wax and honey because of the hives he keeps. He's been watching over me as I watch over Maisy. But I also scent the peppery smell of the twins–in human form.

I veer to the left and race up the mountainside. I don't want to talk to them. I don't want to talk to anyone.

"Catch him, Everest," Darius yells.

Oh, fuck no. I turn again and run faster, but Everest catches me in a flying tackle. The two of us roll together in the snow. His bear is bigger than mine, but mine is ragey from being deprived of his mate, so he can't keep me down.

Except then, Teddy and Darius join the fray, pinning me down in the snow.

I bare my teeth and roar. Everest cuffs my ear with a swipe of his giant paw. I roar again. My three idiot brothers ignore my rage, and drag me up the mountain by my arms and legs.

When we get to my cabin, they throw me on the floor inside and slam the door behind them. They leave Everest outside because of the rule we made that he has to be in human form if he wants to be indoors.

Teddy uses an alpha command on me. "Shift."

I refuse. I'm more dominant than him.

"Shift, fucker," Darius also uses alpha command.

When I remain in bear form, they exchange a look. It takes me longer to decode the look because I'm in bear form, and my thinking is different, but then I catch the acrid scent of fear, and I understand. They're afraid for me.

They think I've turned feral.

Maisy. Maisy. Maisy.

Maybe I have. I haven't taken the Moon Cure since Maisy caught me with it in Vegas. Knowing how much it bothered her, I couldn't take it again.

Which, I guess, leaves me...

Fuck.

I attempt to shift.

The twins try again at the same time, infusing the word, "shift" with alpha command.

It works. I find myself naked on my ass on the cold wooden floor. I ignore the relief on their faces and glare up at them.

"You need a shower." Darius points toward the bathroom. "Now."

I try to speak, but only bear growls come out.

The twins exchange another worried look with each other.

Not wanting to deal with their concern or have a conversation with them, I get to my feet and stomp to the shower. Darius is probably right. I haven't showered in days. I'm sure I smell.

Walking is difficult. I'm not used to walking on two legs, and my feet feel like they're made of lead. My chest feels like an anvil cracked my ribs and remained there, weighing me down.

This is what it's like to live without claiming my mate.

* * *

Maisy

"I have a grande mocha latte with extra whip for Sara," I call, and a tall blonde woman approaches the counter. I recognize her from the front desk at the clinic.

"Thanks, Maisy. I also was going to pick up the to-go order for Nancy?"

"Oh it's right here." I grab it and hand it over. "Nancy the nurse, right? At the clinic?"

"That's right. It's good to see you back."

"Thanks." Most of the townspeople know I was gone. They know the Bad Bear Bros were involved too but don't know the extent of it. Just that there was some bad business I got tangled in because of my dad, and Matthias and his brothers pulled me out.

Matthias. It still hurts to think of his name, but not as bad as it was a few days ago. Like pressing on a bruise or running a finger over a raised scar. The pain is proof I survived.

In the past few days, I've made a lot of progress. Daisy and I finalized the paperwork for me to take half ownership of the cafe. I sent thank yous to the Bad Bear Brothers for rescuing me. Hutch actually got me in touch with the hacker named Kylie, who helped hunt me down after the kidnapping. She also dug into Allen's family, and connected me with the law office that set up the Dankworth trust. I've ordered a marriage certificate sent to them, and once they receive it, I'll come into full ownership of my trust. Most of it is invested, and I intend to keep it that way. I have a meeting scheduled with Paloma to talk about how to make the money grow, and another with Lana, so she can help me with business advice. Everyone's been fully supportive.

I still haven't seen Matthias. My guess is he's gone back to work, but he hasn't been into the cafe.

Sara's his colleague. She would know. And she's still lingering at the counter.

Before I decide whether my heart can take asking about him, she leans in. "Actually, I was hoping to talk to you..."

The cafe is full, but there's no line. Most everyone has settled in with their drinks. I have no idea what Sara would want to talk to me about, but I nod for her to go ahead.

"Have you seen or talked to Dr. Matthias in the past few days?"

I suck in a breath. "No..." I don't have to explain why, do I? No one but Daisy and Missy know about our fake wedding. And no one else needs to know. "I haven't seen him."

"Oh, I thought...someone said they saw you on the Ferris wheel together. They thought you were a couple. Silly small town gossip." She waves it away, and I swallow, trying not to let tears prick my eyes. "It's just that he hasn't shown up to the clinic. He's not answering our calls. Nancy asked a few townspeople, but I don't think anyone's seen him since he got back..."

My skin prickles with warning. That isn't like Matthias. He's rock solid. Dependable as a clock. He never lets anyone down. That's why he was the guy who took the sole responsibility of caring for his mom.

So if he hasn't shown up to work...something's wrong.

I hate the pink princess heart inside me that wants to believe it's because of me. That he cares. That he's as hurt as I am over our ending.

I try to keep my expression neutral. "Have you tried his family? His brothers? Or his mom?"

"No. He didn't have anyone listed for his emergency contact. Nancy had the number for one of his brothers...the one who keeps a garage. Ansel?"

"Axel."

"She called him, and he told her 'Matthias needs to pull his head out of his...rear'." She winces, and I bite back a little smile. Axel doesn't filter for anyone. "That he's unwell, and he'd be 'useless to both man and bear. Whatever that means.'"

He's unwell.

My worry for Matthias ratchets higher. Something's definitely wrong.

I reach into my pocket and finger my wedding ring. I kept it, even though I gave the diamond necklace back.

If Matthias is in trouble, would he want to see me?

"I...I'll make some calls," I tell her.

But that doesn't feel right.

"No, I'll go by his place."

"Thank you. Nancy's working doubles, and I'm calling in every favor to get some part time help, but we really need him."

I've never been to Matthias' cabin. Before our date, before Vegas, we barely interacted. Still, something gives the authority to feel I have the right to go to his place uninvited.

More than the fact that I'm his legal wife. It's that I suspect—no, I'm certain—that Matthias' absence is about me. He's unwell because of me. I try to remember what he explained when he was giving me his doctorly summary on the mating of his species.

If a male shifter finds his mate but doesn't claim her, he can go moon mad.

Is Matthias going moon mad without me? But no, he has his Moon Cure. Except...he told me he wouldn't take it if it bothered me.

Oh God.

He said when a shifter went feral, they'd have to be put down.

Put down.

My fear spikes higher.

Matthias is the sort of man who is ethical to a fault. If he's honoring my wishes and not taking Moon Cure and also not making contact with me, then I need to be the one to go to him.

Because Matthias belongs to me.

That thought startles me, but it feels true. Maybe he's right, maybe this thing between us is just biology, but to me, it feels like love. Like he's the most important person in the world to me, and if he's hurt, I'm hurt. That it's my responsibility, right, and privilege to go and check on him and make sure he's okay.

I slip the wedding ring back on my finger and take off my smock.

Biology or love, Matthias is mine. He's always been mine, whether he claimed me or not. And I won't let him die.

* * *

Matthias

I take a shower, leaving the water cold, hoping to shock myself into feeling better. Or at least different. Anything but this. The pain of knowing I hurt my mate kills me.

When I get out and put some clothes on, I find the twins haven't left. Teddy's built a fire in my fireplace, and Darius is frying a slab of salmon on the stove.

The scent of freshly cooked fish re-wakens my bear, though, and I trip, half shifting to bear form and falling to my knees before gaining control again.

"Matthias, what the fuck?" Darius demands twisting from the stove. "You've nearly lost it, man."

"Give him some food," Teddy directs, holding a plate out.

Darius slides half the salmon steak onto a plate, and Teddy puts it on the table, helping me sit.

My hands transform to claws as I snatch up the food, my fangs lengthening to chew. The fish tastes amazing. I must have forgotten to eat anything these past few days. I scarf down my plate, and hunch my back to lower my head and lick it clean.

When I look up, Teddy and Darius are exchanging glances.

"What?" It comes out more of a grunt.

"I've never seen you like this," Teddy says.

"You look bad, man."

I growl and keep licking my plate clean. Then I drop it and wipe a hand across my mouth. It feels weird being in man form. But it's nice having opposable thumbs. My belly is full, even though my upper chest cavity feels empty. I try to grunt, "Thank you" but it comes out as a bear growl.

Still, Darius gets the meaning. "Anytime. You'd do the same for us."

"Hell, you have." Teddy leans back in his chair, propping it on two back legs. "I never thought I'd see you acting like..."

"Like us," Darius says. I know they're in sync when they stop fighting and start finishing each other's sentences.

But it's annoying. I want them to fight. I want to fight them, use up this useless energy crawling beneath my skin.

Maisy Maisy Maisy—

"Matthias!"

My ears ring like Teddy's been calling my name for some time.

"You need to get it together," he says. "You're going feral."

Darius says, "You're better than this."

I shrug. What does it matter? I lost Maisy.

"Mom's worried about you." Darius plays the guilt card. "She told us about the shifter cancer."

I pause at that. They know?

"You shouldn't have taken all of that on yourself, Matthias," Darius says.

"Yeah," Teddy agrees. "But she still needs you. What if she comes out of remission?"

"If you don't care about us, or Mom, think of Maisy. You don't want her to see you like this."

"She's not going to. See me."

"Why not? She's your mate."

"Don't deserve her." What Axel told me rings true.

"You think I deserve Paloma?" Darius asks. "Do you think he deserves Lana?" He points to Teddy, who's shaking his head.

"We mated up. There's nothing we could do to deserve our mates. They just love us, and we let their love make us better."

"It's not that we earn it...it's more that we recognize the version of us that they love, and we choose to be that version every day."

"Can't." If I get close to Maisy, I'll hurt her. And I won't allow that.

So I have to stay away.

Darius closes his eyes. Teddy growls, "Were we this stupid?"

"You were," Darius says.

"Shut up."

Both of them peer at me. Outside, I see Everest's bulk just out the window, his rounded bear ears perked up. Even in bear form, he looks worried.

If I don't get a hold of myself, I'm going to lose my humanity. That's why my brothers are so afraid.

But Maisy's gone. And all I can think is, *Maybe it's easier to let the bear take me.*

Chapter Twenty-Four

M *aisy*

I drive up Bad Bear Mountain. I know where Lana and Teddy live. I also know which property is Darius, Paloma and Wren's. Both of them have built new, gorgeous mountain homes in the past few years.

I also know that threaded through the woods are the older cabins where each brother lives, but I don't know which one is Matthias.

Still, I drive straight up the mountain, somehow certain that I'll figure it out.

I scream and throw on the brakes when a giant, polar-grizzly leaps in front of the car, waving its giant paws. My Subaru is made for snow, but it still skids at the sudden stop.

The bear leaps toward the rear of my car and braces against it to stop the skid.

"Everest! " I open my door to look back at him. "What's wrong? Is it Matthias?" My fear spikes again.

He nods his head and starts loping forward on the road.

I step on the gas, making the Subaru fishtail again. I'm

hoping he's leading me to the cabin. When he heads off-road and plunges into the woods, I hope that he's on a road, so I don't get stuck in a ditch.

He points again. I round the bend and see an adorable cabin nestled in the trees. The windows glow with firelight, and I see figures in the windows.

"Is this it?"

Everest paws at my door.

I skid to a stop. Okay, I guess this is it.

I throw open my door and jog to the cabin. There is a freshly tromped path of bear tracks and human boots through the snow, as well as the imprint of something large being dragged.

Matthias! Oh, God.

I throw the door open without knocking, fear gripping my throat.

Matthias' head jerks up from where it rested in his hands. He's sitting at the kitchen table while his brothers stand over him.

He lurches from the chair toward me. His clothes rip and shred as he changes from man to bear midair.

Darius and Teddy both grab his arms to keep him from reaching me.

"Whoa! No, Matthias! You'll hurt her. Shift back," Darius yells.

"*Shift,* Matthias," Teddy commands.

Their agitation and obvious fear only increase mine.

"Let him go!" I cry out, running to him.

They don't release him, but I put my hand on his chest, over his heart. "Hey," I say softly. "What's wrong?"

He lets out a long bear-warble. It makes the hair on the back of my neck raise.

"Can you shift back?" I ask gently.

He roars and shakes his head, jerking away from his brothers and knocking me back in the process.

"No, Matthias!" The twins tackle him to the ground.

I scream.

What can I do?

"The bear wants to mark her," Teddy mutters.

"Fuck. He's too wild. He's gonna hurt her." Darius straddles Matthias' chest to hold him down on the ground.

I spy his black doctor's bag on the hearth. The Moon Cure! I run for it and dump the contents onto the sofa with shaking hands.

Syringe. Vial. Rubber strap. "Is this what you need?" I hold them up to show Matthias.

He roars.

"What is that?" Darius asks.

I yank off my coat, so I'm less restricted. "A medicine he developed to keep from going moon mad. He calls it Moon Cure."

"Hell, I didn't know anything about this. Did you?" Teddy looks at his twin, who shakes his head.

I've never filled a syringe before. Never used a needle, but I figure it out. I'm a capable person, and Matthias needs me.

I walk over to him, my heart in my throat. Then I realize he's covered in fur. I have no idea where his veins would be. Well, I'll just have to use a big muscle, then. I drop to my knees, jab the needle into his quad, and depress the plunger.

He lets out a deep, low grumble that goes on for several seconds.

Darius gets off his brother, who has stopped fighting. He takes the syringe from me and sniffs it, then hands it to Teddy.

I try to catch Matthias' eye, but his giant bear head

turns away from me, like he's ashamed. He rumbles some more.

My heart thuds. Should he have transformed by now? How long does it take to work? Was I too late?

A tear drips down my nose.

Matthias' head jerks around, his nose twitching like he smelled my tear. He opens his giant jaws, and then his body contorts.

I gasp as I hear the sound of popping joints, but it's okay. Matthias is transforming back to a man.

A very naked man.

A gorgeous, naked man who belongs to me.

"Thank fuck," Teddy murmurs. He and Darius move back to give him room.

Matthias sits up, leaning back on his hands like he's weak and stares at me, panting.

"So...it worked?" I croak.

He nods, his eyes shadowed. "I'm sorry. I...I didn't want to take it anymore. You didn't like it," he explains.

Tears prick my eyes. "I don't want you to turn feral, Matthias."

"Seems like you got this, brother," Teddy mutters. "Maisy, call Everest if he shifts again."

I nod, and the twins leave the cabin, giving us privacy.

He looks at me. His gaze snags on the wedding ring I put back on.

I look at his hand to see he's still wearing his too. My breath catches.

"What do you want, Maisy?"

"I want you to claim me," I whisper.

His eyes turn red, and he blinks hard. "You do?" His voice sounds rough. He starts to reach for me as I speak.

"But..."

He freezes. "Yes?"

"Not if you don't want me. I don't want to be with someone who doesn't want me. Or love me."

"Maisy, beautiful." He's in motion now, reaching for me, lifting me to straddle his waist. "You're all I want. Fuck, is that how I screwed this up? I made you think I didn't want you?"

I suck on my lower lip and nod.

"Gah! That's why you didn't like hearing it was a biological attraction." He smacks his forehead with the heel of his hand. "I'm such an idiot. My explanation must've been the least romantic thing you'd ever heard."

"Yes. It was."

"Maisy, you're everything to me. I adore you. I'm obsessed with you. You're the only female I've ever wanted or ever will want. And I'm sorry I made you think anything other than that."

"But is that all just biology?"

Matthias leans his forehead against mine. "No, sweetheart," he murmurs. "Science soothes me. Reducing transcendent experiences to scientific or medical explanations helps me think I can control them, but, of course, I can't. And my scientific explanation hurt your feelings. I'm so sorry."

"But if you want me, why didn't you claim me?"

Matthias' expression takes on that stoic look I've come to recognize. The one he wore when he talked about keeping his mother's illness a secret from the entire family and carrying the burden all on his own. "It wouldn't be fair to you. You're young. Barely an adult. You hadn't even experimented with another man—not a date or even a kiss. How could I trap you into a lifelong mating before you even had a chance to experience life?"

My lips part in shock.

That's why he didn't want to mate me? Not that I wasn't experienced enough for him, but this was Matthias' altruism coming out. The tight bands that had been constricting my heart since the day I left Las Vegas burst open. My chest fills with warm light.

Still, I want to be sure I understand. I tilt my head. "So you were... were protecting me...from yourself?"

* * *

Matthias

It feels so incredible to have my mate in my arms again. Her caramel and cinnamon scent soothe my bear. It's a miracle I didn't expect.

"Yes, beautiful. I was afraid I'd steamroll you. I know I'm a lot. Especially in bed. You have no idea the filthy things I want to do to you."

Far from being taken aback, my mate smiles and frames my face with her hands. She drops her voice into a sexy purr. "I want you to do those filthy things to me."

My dick lengthens under her lap. I grip her ass and pull her closer, a possessive twinge returning to my behavior.

She lowers her lips and slides them across mine, and I want to weep from the pleasure of it. The sweetness.

"Did you ever stop to consider that maybe I wasn't out experimenting with other guys because I was waiting for you to claim me? I might have read a gazillion sexy books, but I was fantasizing about you to experience the real thing. I mean, here you are, and yet, you're the guy who's explaining away our entire attraction to biology."

I groan and lean my forehead against hers again. She will probably never let me live that one down.

She continues, "Wouldn't it stand to reason that if I'm your mate, my biology wouldn't allow me to be interested in another man?"

I blink. "Well, yes, I guess that would make sense."

"Listen, here's the only way this is going to work."

My heart pounds. I'm usually the dom. The one in control. Before I knew Maisy was my mate, I made females beg and plead for more. Even with Maisy, I've been the one setting the rules in our relationship or non-relationship.

It's unnerving to be the one prepared to beg now.

"I'm either your equal and able to make my own decisions about who I want to be with and whether I want to be with you, or I'm out. You're either going to let me choose, or you're treating me like I'm a child, and I'm not going to be with someone who doesn't value me or trust me to make up my own mind."

I suck in a breath, finally understanding how badly I fucked up.

I was trying to protect her from my controlling, dominant, all-consuming side. Trying to protect her from all the dark and filthy things I want to do with her. I tried not to wield undue influence on a female so much younger than I am. But it was that very paternalism that offended her.

I thought I was leaving space for her to have a choice. But in reality, I took a choice away from her. I didn't let her choose.

I clear my throat. "I'm sorry, Maisy. I took your choice from you, and that was wrong. You are my equal. Absolutely."

"So I get to choose?"

"Of course." My heart's still pounding. She's here, on my lap, in my arms, but she could still tell me it's off. She could still walk away like she did in Las Vegas.

"Do you trust me?"

"With my whole heart."

Her expression softens at my choice of words. Yes, I included my heart, and I wasn't even talking about the organ that pumps blood through the body.

"I choose you."

My eyes get wet. The lump in my throat won't go away.

"I choose you," I say. "My heart chooses you. My mind chooses you. My soul chooses you. My bear chooses you. My body chooses you." I try to cover all my bases, so she'll never doubt my love again.

"You," she whispers, her eyes glittering with tears, too.

"You." A smile cracks my face for the first time in a week. It feels like it might break. No, wait. That's the cage around my heart splintering open. I kiss her, hard. "Yeah?" I ask when I pull away, and she's breathless.

She smiles back and nods. "Yeah. Only you. It's always been you."

I capture the back of her head with my palm and pull her down on top of me then log roll us until she's on her back, pinned beneath me.

"Once I mark you, I'll never let you go," I warn.

She flushes, but her expression is pure pleasure. "Promise?"

Chapter Twenty-Five

M *aisy*

Matthias' eyes glow electric blue. His fangs look long and sharp and deliciously dangerous.

"Last chance to run," he warns as he yanks my sweater off over my head. I toe off the boots I am still wearing, trying to aid him in his endeavor to get me naked.

"I'm not running."

He unhooks my bra. "I won't be gentle."

"Bring it, Bear Daddy."

He arches a decidedly dommy brow. "Am I your bear daddy?" He strips off my jeans and panties.

I flush. "That's what I call you in my head."

His grin is feral. "I like it." He lifts his chin toward the fireplace. "Now, crawl."

It takes me a moment to realize what he wants, but then I scramble up onto all fours. He gives my ass a sharp slap. "Over to the rug by the fire where I'm going to fuck you senseless."

Fuck me...senseless. Sounds like a plan to me!

As I crawl to the fireplace, he rumbles his approval and gives the coffee table and sofa a hard shove back, clearing the floor for us. He grabs one of the pillows from the sofa and sets it beside me.

I wait on all fours on the rug by the fire. "What did the flame say to his buddies after he fell in love?"

"Hmm." Matthias' large hands settle on my waist, and he lets out another bear rumble of approval. "What?"

I twist to look over my shoulder at him. "I found my perfect match!"

He throws back his head and lets out a laugh.

I love in control, doctor-dommy Matthias, but seeing him happy and free like this? I fall in love all over again. Hard.

He strokes his palms all over my body–up and down my sides, around my ass, cupping my breasts. "I love you, Maisy," he murmurs.

I let his words soak in. The ones I needed to hear back in Vegas, instead of, "it's just biology."

"Claim me."

His bear growls. He slaps my ass. "You're making it hard for me to stay in control."

"Claim me," I repeat. I want this. I want this more than I've wanted anything in my life. Matthias is my mate. He's right–I've known it for as long as he has.

He continues to slap my ass, alternating right and left cheeks, exciting me with the spanking. With his dominance.

I instantly get wet. *Thank you, Bear Daddy.*

Now that we've established that I'm his equal, I'm more than happy to let him lead. Especially in bed.

Or on my knees on the floor in front of the fire, as it may be.

He strokes between my legs, and I moan softly at the touch. "Put the pillow under your chest, beautiful."

I obey, putting the pillow under my breasts, so I'm now in a form of "puppy pose" with my ass higher than my chest.

Matthias curses. "You are so hot, Maisy." He slaps my ass again, a little harder this time. "How will I ever let you out of the bedroom?" He strokes his palm around my ass.

I let out a puff of laughter. "You don't have to."

"Careful, beautiful," he rumbles. "I might take you up on that."

"Take me now, Bear Daddy."

"Maisy..." He groans as he rubs the head of his cock through my juices. "I'm going to fuck you day and night."

He eases into me. The angle is delicious–his cock goes in deep. I feel objectified. Beautiful. He pulls back and pushes back in, going slowly. Letting me get used to his size.

When he brings the pad of his finger in front of my hips to circle over my clit, I moan my appreciation.

"Fuck, Maisy." He grips my waist with bruising force. He pushes in harder. "Fuck." He starts to gain speed with his thrusts. "I wanted to take my time with you, but I..."

"Claim me," I repeat.

I so want this. All the rough, kinky sex he thought I wasn't ready for.

"Maisy...Maisy. Maisy–"

He's losing control, and I love it. I love that I'm the one who makes him lose control.

"Give it to me, Bear Daddy," I tease.

He growls, pounding into me now.

It's too much, but I love it. Turns out, I like a bit of pain as much as he likes delivering it. *I found my perfect match.*

I laugh to myself at the dumb dad joke because now it's about me. About us.

"Maisy...Maisy, fuck."

Matthias releases my hip with one hand to rub my clit again. This time, it's enough to send me over. I shriek as my internal muscles start pulsing in a fast, hard release.

Matthias lets out a bear snarl and shoves deep, coming inside me. His growl sends chills up my spine. He would never hurt me, so the fear turns to a thrill. There's a beast at my back, and I belong to him.

Then his arm is around me, holding me fast. For a moment he presses his lips to the muscle between my neck and shoulder. He growls again, and I get that he's asking me.

"Do it," I whisper.

He clamps onto my neck so fast, I don't feel anything for a moment. His lips are fastened on my skin. My muscle cramps–his fangs are deep in my skin.

"Mine," he growls. Pain flares through me, and I collapse. Only his arm holds me up.

But my smile is huge, stretching my face. He did it. I'm claimed.

He licks my skin, lapping up blood, I realize. His growl is more of a purr. My body is boneless in the aftermath of his bite and my orgasm. I'm floating, weightless in his hold.

He turns me over and licks my face. Licking up my tears.

"Wife." The concerned note in his voice makes me blink at him. He's searching my face. His own expression is the familiar Dr. Hunk one I know and love—calm and in control. "You okay?"

"Mmmhmmm."

"You're high on neurochemicals." He chuckles and lifts me into his arms. "I should've done this on the bed."

"No." My knees are red from taking his weight. Still. "I wouldn't have it any other way." I touch his lips, inhaling his delicious scent. I'm coated in it now. I hope I smell sandal-wood everywhere I go. "Mate."

"Mate." He nips my fingers. His lips are soft and strong. He carries me to his bed, where he checks me over. After I drink some water and take some pain pills, he lays down and pulls me against him. I snuggle up to him, and it feels so right.

I feel like I have someone who will be my rock. Someone who will share my hopes and fears, who will hold me when I cry and laugh at my bad jokes.

Someone who sees the real me. Someone who will never let me go.

"Thank you," I whisper.

"No, sweet wife. Thank you."

Chapter Twenty-Six

Maisy

I never celebrated Valentine's day. I never had a date, never had plans other than telling cafe customers about our signature red velvet latte made with sweet cream and red sparkling sugar. I'd never been kissed.

This year, everything's different.

I stand in front of my bedroom's full-length mirror, straightening the collar of my off-the shoulder wedding dress. The neckline shows off my diamond necklace and mating mark, and I wouldn't have it any other way.

My ring finger feels bare without my wedding band, though.

There's a knock on my door, and before I'm finished murmuring "come in," Daisy sails through.

"Happy birthday, darling girl!" she cries. "It's a gorgeous day." She sets a bright yellow mug of coffee on my dresser then turns and gets a good look at me. Her breath catches. "Oh my."

"Daisy?" My grandmother has recovered most of her

energy, but she's changed. She seems...softer. She cries more easily. Like now. Her face fills with wonder, and her eyes grow glassy with tears.

"Darling girl," she whispers. "You look stunning."

I cross the room to take both her hands, holding tight in case she falls.

"Oh, my Maisy." She squeezes my hand with strong fingers. "You're all grown up."

It takes a moment to stop my lip from wobbling. Missy did my makeup, and there's no way I'm messing it up. "Will you zip me?"

She spends the next few minutes fussing over my gown. She's in a stunning dress of her own, bright turquoise with pops of yellow and a daisy pin. Lana had it made by an up-and-coming designer.

We both have coats that match our gowns.

"There, all set. Oh, you look like a snow queen."

I glance at the mirror. Missy did use a lot of shimmer on my cheeks and eyelids. I look ethereal.

"Thanks for walking me down the aisle."

I asked Daisy to walk me down the aisle. I wouldn't want Allen here. Besides, Matthias told me he's been mind-wiped by a vampire and is now living his best life as a waiter in Vancouver.

"Of course. I've never seen a more beautiful bride. If your mom could see you now... but of course she's looking down on you from heaven."

"Don't make me cry." I tip my head up and blink my tears back.

Outside our door, someone honks a horn.

"That's our ride. Before we go, let me say this." She cups my face between her hands. "I never thought there'd be a man who deserves you, but you found him. That man won't ever leave you lonely. I swear he looks at you like you're his whole world. I know when my time is done that he'll take care of you."

"Stop." I sniffle. "You're living a long time. Don't you want to hold your great-grandbabies?"

Our ride honks the horn again.

Daisy opens the door and hollers, "All right, keep your shirt on," at Axel, who's parked by our mailbox in one of his project hot rods, a sky blue convertible. Even though the air is frosty, he has the top down. He hops out, swinging his long hair like a K-pop star. All his tattoos are hidden under his tux, so he looks very conventional and dashing, like a Jane Austen hero.

"Daisy." He bows low as he opens the door for her. "You're looking lovely."

"Yes, thank you, young man. I feel sixty-two again."

"Maisy, I have something for you." He grabs a black velvet box and presents me with a sparkling tiara. "One last touch." He sets it on my head as I play with the diamonds on my necklace, feeling breathless. "Perfect."

I'm so happy I can't speak. I let him help me into the front seat.

"Let's get this show on the road." From the back, Daisy slaps her hand against the driver's seat.

The cold air rushes by us, but we have such a short drive it's like being in a horse-drawn sleigh. I can feel my cheeks glowing pink.

While Daisy's busy humming "Jingle Bells," I drop my voice to a murmur to ask Axel, "Is Missy already there?"

Axel nods. "I dropped her off earlier."

I study his face closely. Matthias told me he had a thing for Missy. I haven't told Missy yet. She's always acted like she doesn't like Axel. Someday soon, I'm going to get to the bottom of their relationship. But not today. Today's for me.

Me and my husband.

Axel drops us off at the end of Main Street, right where a carpet of white rose petals begin. The whole town stretches before us. The Leaky Bucket on one side, the Trading Post on the other. Our cafe beyond that, with the Winterfest Ferris wheel rising behind it.

The path of rose petals ends at a stage flanked by some impressive ice statues. That's where Matthias is waiting in his white tux.

"Ready?" Daisy offers me her arm. We stroll down the street, only to be joined by Everest in bear form. He's closed his teeth around the handle of a white wicker basket. Inside the basket is a velvety white pillow holding our two wedding rings. He's taking the role of ring-bearer very seriously. He even has a sky-blue bowtie around his neck to match the sky-blue dresses and tuxes (or kilts) our bridal party is wearing.

As soon as Daisy and I step onto the carpet of rose petals, the triplets strike up the bagpipes. The blast of sound is impressive. I've never heard "Love Me Tender" done so... loudly.

That's when people start pouring out of Daisy Day and the Beary Nice Bookstore. There's Old Man Luther, Sara, and Nancy from the clinic. Even Abe leaves his bar to stand on the porch of the Leaky Bucket. It looks like the whole town's turned out to watch me walk down the aisle to Matthias.

Missy, Lana, and Paloma appear and take their place in front of me as bridesmaids. As of two weeks ago, Lana, Paloma, and I are officially in business together. They are funding the cafe's expansion, and using my business as a test case for their non-profit that helps female, queer, and POC entrepreneurs. With their help, I've already filed permits for the cafe's expansion.

My whole life has been transformed. I feel like I'm dreaming, like I've stepped inside a holiday movie—a cozy one that always has a happy ending.

My happy ending comes with a bite mark on my shoulder and a diamond necklace that's secretly a collar. And an Elvis soundtrack performed with bagpipes. I think the triplets are trying to play "Can't Help Falling in Love with You." But I wouldn't have it any other way.

Teddy and Lana then Darius and Paloma walk down the aisle. Axel offers his arm to Missy, and I hold my breath, but she takes it with a regal nod and holds her head high as he escorts her to the stage.

They look good together. Maybe I'll tell her that tomorrow.

Everest prowls down the aisle, and then it's Daisy's and my turn.

People murmur their congratulations as I pass.

"You got a good one. About time someone locked Dr. Hunk down," Terri from Trading post calls. Abe tips his Stetson to me.

Jasmine Waters holds Oliver back as he reaches down, takes fistfuls of rose petals in his chubby toddler hands, and throws them in the air as I pass.

That's when I look up and see Matthias. He's on stage staring down at me, and suddenly we're the only two people in the world. We could be back in the playroom, with me crawling to him.

Maybe later tonight.

The bite on my neck throbs, and I pray I don't soak through my sky blue panties before the vows are done.

We pass the huge ice sculptures–they're in the shape of bears, of course–and climb the stage stairs to the altar. Daisy takes her place next to Winnie, Matthias' mom. They both got an online certificate, so they could officiate the wedding. They're good friends, and Winnie's been busy making us feel like part of the family. "You ready to have six wild brothers-in-law?" Matthias asked me yesterday. I told him that at least two of them had awesome mates. "Two down, five to go," Matthias muttered.

"Three down," I corrected.

Now he takes my hand and warms it between his large ones. Never in my wildest dreams would I have imagined this moment.

Matthias leans down. "Why did the groom wear extra socks on his wedding day?"

I know the answer, but I ask, "Why?" My cheeks are sore from smiling.

Matthias winks. "In case he got cold feet."

"Dearly beloved," Winnie says. She and Daisy take turns prompting us through the vows. I can barely hear what they're saying. I'm vibrating with excitement, just standing in the circle of my husband's arms.

"Maisy Stark has a nice *ring* to it," he whispers as he slips the wedding band back on my finger. Back where it belongs.

"Why did the groom stand on the left during the wedding ceremony?" I ask, and he answers, "Because his bride was always right."

"I now pronounce you the king and queen of Winterfest!" Daisy shouts. "And also married!"

Everyone erupts into applause.

"You may kiss the bride," Winnie adds, but Matthias is

already sweeping me into the crook of his arm. He tips me back and our lips meet.

And then the triplets are there, laughing, and putting a silver crown on Matthias' head. I'm already wearing mine.

"Three cheers for Maisy and Matthias Stark!" Sara calls. "Hip hip, hooray!" the whole town shouts loud enough to echo off the mountain.

I'm crying with happiness. There's no hope for my makeup now.

"Happy birthday, wife. Did I get you what you wanted?"

"Yes." I cup his face and whisper against his mouth. "You."

* * *

We hope you've enjoyed *Alpha's Mate*. If you did, we would so appreciate your review. They make a huge difference to the authors.

If you haven't read Darius and Paloma's book, check out *Alpha's Claim*.

To read Teddy and Lana's book, *Alpha's Rescue*, click here.

Did you know you can buy direct from Renee & Lee? Get early access to new books, special editions, and heavily discounted bundles. Use this coupon for an additional 10% discount on your entire order - **10READER or** click here **https://midnightromanceshop.com/ discount/10READER**

Want FREE books?

Go to **http://subscribepage.com/alphastemp** to sign up for Renee Rose's newsletter and receive free books. In addition to the free stories and bonus material, you will also get special pricing, exclusive previews and news of new releases.

Did you know you can buy direct from Renee Rose? Get signed books, special editions, and heavily discounted bundles. Use this coupon for an additional 10% discount on your entire order - **READER10** or go here https://shop.reneeroseromance.com/discount/READER10

Download a free Lee Savino book from www. leesavino.com

Did you know you can buy direct from Lee Savino? Get special editions and heavily discounted bundles. Use this coupon for an additional 10% discount on your entire order - **READER10 or** click here **https://leesavino. myshopify.com/discount/READER10**

Other Titles by Renee Rose

Paranormal

Werewolves of Wall Street

Big Bad Boss: Midnight

Big Bad Boss: Moon Mad

Big Bad Boss: Marked

Big Bad Boss: Mated

Big Bad Bully

Wolf Ridge High Series

Alpha Bully

Alpha Knight

Step Alpha

Alpha King

Alpha Varsity

Bad Boy Alphas Series

Alpha's Temptation

Alpha's Danger

Alpha's Prize

Alpha's Challenge

Alpha's Obsession

Alpha's Desire

Alpha's War

Alpha's Mission

Wolf Ranch Series

Rough

Wild

Feral

Savage

Fierce

Ruthless

Primal

Rugged

Ravenous

Dangerous

Other Paranormal

Claimed by the Storm

Contemporary
Chicago Sin

Den of Sins

Rooted in Sin

Made Men Series

Don't Tease Me

Don't Tempt Me

Don't Make Me

Chicago Bratva

"Prelude" in Black Light: Roulette War

The Director

The Fixer

"Owned" in Black Light: Roulette Rematch

The Enforcer

The Soldier

The Hacker

The Bookie

The Cleaner

The Player

The Gatekeeper

Alpha Mountain

Hero

Rebel

Warrior

Vegas Underground Mafia Romance

King of Diamonds

Mafia Daddy

Jack of Spades

Ace of Hearts

Joker's Wild

His Queen of Clubs

Dead Man's Hand

Wild Card

Master Me Series

Her Royal Master

Yes, Doctor

Her Russian Master

His Human Prisoner

Training His Human

His Human Rebel

His Human Vessel

His Mate and Master

Zandian Pet

Their Zandian Mate

His Human Possession

Zandian Brides

Night of the Zandians

Bought by the Zandians

Mastered by the Zandians

Zandian Lights

Kept by the Zandian

Claimed by the Zandian

Stolen by the Zandian

Rescued by the Zandian

Other Sci-Fi

The Hand of Vengeance

Her Alien Masters

Also by Lee Savino

Paranormal romance

The Berserker Saga and Berserker Brides (menage werewolves)

These fierce warriors will stop at nothing to claim their mates.

Draekons (Dragons in Exile) with Lili Zander (menage alien dragons)

Crashed spaceship. Prison planet. Two big, hulking, bronzed aliens who turn into dragons. The best part? The dragons insist I'm their mate.

Bad Boy Alphas with Renee Rose (bad boy werewolves)

Never ever date a werewolf.

Tsenturion Masters with Golden Angel

Who knew my e-reader was a portal to another galaxy? Now I'm stuck with a fierce alien commander who wants to claim me as his own.

Contemporary Romance

Royal Bad Boy

I'm not falling in love with my arrogant, annoying, sex god boss. Nope. No way.

Royally Fake Fiancé

The Duke of New Arcadia has an image problem only a fiancé can fix. And I'm the lucky lady he's chosen to play Cinderella.

Beauty & The Lumberjacks

After this logging season, I'm giving up sex. For...reasons.

Her Marine Daddy

My hot Marine hero wants me to call him daddy...

Her Dueling Daddies

Two daddies are better than one.

Innocence: dark mafia romance with Stasia Black

I'm the king of the criminal underworld. I always get what I want. And she is my obsession.

Beauty's Beast: a dark romance with Stasia Black

Years ago, Daphne's father stole from me. Now it's time for her to pay her family's debt...with her body.

About Renee Rose

USA TODAY BESTSELLING AUTHOR RENEE ROSE loves a dominant, dirty-talking alpha hero! She's sold over two million copies of steamy romance with varying levels of kink. Her books have been featured in USA Today's *Happily Ever After* and *Popsugar*. Named Eroticon USA's Next Top Erotic Author in 2013, she has also won *Spunky and Sassy's* Favorite Sci-Fi and Anthology author, *The Romance Reviews* Best Historical Romance, and has hit the *USA Today* list fifteen times with her Bad Boy Alphas, Chicago Bratva, and Wolf Ranch series.

Renee loves to connect with readers!
www.reneeroseromance.com
reneeroseauthor@gmail.com

facebook.com/reneeroseromance
instagram.com/reneeroseromance
bookbub.com/authors/renee-rose
goodreads.com/ReneeRose

About Lee Savino

Lee Savino is a USA today bestselling author, mom and chocoholic.

Warning: Do not read her Berserker series, or you will be addicted to the huge, dominant warriors who will stop at nothing to claim their mates.

I repeat: Do. Not. Read. The Berserker Saga.

Download a free book from www.leesavino.com (don't read that either. Too much hot, sexy lovin').